IF

The 4th Storybook

by TS Caladan

Edited by TS Caladan

Art Design by TS Caladan

Published by TWB Press; https://www.twbpress.com

ISBN: 978-1-959768-94-4

THE 33 STORIES:

1 Peep and the Tree of Evil.............................1

2 The Great Insect Rebellion.........................5

3 The Aurora is God....................................13

4 Pandragon of Prague................................19

5 Noseferatu..31

6 The Family Curse.....................................39

7 Jason and the Harpies...............................51

8 Robin Hoodlum.......................................57

9 IF Clark Kent was Batman & Bruce Wayne
was Superman...63

10 What Happened to Brainiac 5?..................71

11 The 7 Faces of Doctor No........................75

12 Plans 1 – 8 from Outer Space...................77

13 Forbidden Moon....................................79

14 The Day Mars Stood Still.........................85

15 Zorro, Lost in Space 95

16 Sungate..103

17 RATAVA...107

18 A Boy and his Cat*................................111

19 The Pittsburgh Experiment.....................125

20 Day of the Dead Living..........................131

21 The Mirror of Dorian White....................137

22 Field of Nightmares...............................147

23 League of their Own..............................155

24 Greatest Tennis Player of All Time............161

25 Flog..169

26 Story of Alfred E. Neuman......................173

27 Pets..179

28 Jose..181
29 Homecoming................................185
30 The Wrong Door............................195
31 Saved..199
32 The Death Chair............................201
33 Where are you going?....................205
Author's comments on the 33 Stories..............209

1 Peep and the Tree of Evil

"What IF…what would happen if one day, one day, I would be truly free? My Master said I would live forever, see the beautiful world around me flourish over many years from a tree, and I held the most important job in the world: I was the Keeper of Evil. Because of me, the Earth was safe from major disasters, plagues and great wars."

Peep was a mere elf, a woodland elf, who had many friends, originally. He was once very attractive, as the story goes, with a lovely face and slim body only 4-foot in height. He was well-liked and was always invited to parties held by other elves, pixies and fairies. Those were days long before the privilege, the employment (or was it his *imprisonment* inside the Tree of Evil?).

He made a deal with the Dark Master of the Grove. Peep was popular with many creatures of the forest and Grove, but he wanted much more than popularity or even fame. The small elf desired power! Peep wanted to rise above the crowd and *fly free!* He wanted to matter and do something GREAT. He knew he was different than other elves and he was meant for fantastic things, to rule, to make decisions and sit alongside the gods of heaven and Earth! Peep, tiny mortal Peep, believed he was his soul and his spirit-energy was divine and angelic and perfect. Peep wanted to live forever, and would sell his soul to do so. Because of his hubris, because of his supreme ego, Peep was offered a very important job by the Grove Master that he could not refuse: He agreed to forever live in the Tree of Evil – that was the deal. "Peep was a savior, and had saved the planet from terrible disasters that could have happened, but didn't." Or, was the Grove Master lying through his sharp teeth?

The Tree of Evil needed a life to do its magic. Peep was its heart and soul and was transformed in the process. The pretty, popular elf soaked up the darkness and grime of horror and terror in the tree trunk's blood and morphed over time into a hideous, dwarf creature!

His stay in the Tree of Evil was not what the elf with high hopes wanted or thought it would be. He thought the tree was a huge castle, his domain where he would rule. Peep believed he'd have servants and things at his command. No. He was trapped within the close quarters of a tree trunk, a hard/black tree trunk whose wood dripped with pure EVIL.

So much so that Peep changed into a monster, a devil. He grew horns, not unlike the Grove Master, only smaller. The transformation was not sudden, it took years. This was not what the elf bargained for: to see a fabulous world change seasons, day after day, year after year, while he was tightly locked inside the bark of a cursed tree?

Even if the small elf truly held back the tide, or the planet, from Evil (he thought), *Was it all worth it? I appear as a hero to no one. Who knows what I have done, if I have really done what the Master said? Where is my gain, my reward? I surely thought the job would come to an end and possibly another would take my place? I believed I would live at some point…free. Even PAID, at some point for what I've done, for my service? But? But, nothing in all this time? Not a word from the Grove Master? What madness is this? I know it's the Tree of Evil and I agreed…but, still. Won't someone or something end my misery? I see a sweet, tender world change seasons. But, what about me? PEEP! I want with all my heart to be released, free! Help!*

Sometimes, miracles happen. Sometimes, small voices are heard and pleas for help are answered. Prayers answered positively. At some point in time, eternities end. Pain and suffering ends, as it was in the case of the elf, Peep, who was demonized by an evil tree and an evil Master. But was all as it seemed?

Peep was given the power he desired, with

conditions: He could live any life he chose, but he would die a natural death and not live forever. The elf agreed and was excited. Anything he wanted? It took time to decide. Now he knew for sure and he could not have been happier. His wishes came true: He didn't want to be a woodland elf after seeing human society. He became a modern, young man named Peter Hendrix, after he ripped himself away from a dissolved evil tree.

You might think the Grove Master had a change of heart and felt sympathy for his trapped minion? No. The GM lied. Peep was needed to broadcast Evil from the Tree, not keep the world protected from harm. Peep, unknowingly, greatly harmed the planet and was no hero. Even now, his release was not any type of kind gesture. It was an illusion that the Tree of Evil dissolved into nothing. No. EVIL seeped through the ground, through water systems, in plants, forests, rivers, in the air, throughout animals, and people. And especially, the insects.

2 The Great Insect Rebellion

IF bugs stood up on two legs.

It all started when insects realized that they could stand-up. Not all, but many insect species suddenly found that they could *balance upright and stand tall.* This one small act created a Revolution, an Atomic Bomb, among insects on a planetary scale! You see, once one 6-legged bug did it, then, soon, all the bugs did it. It was the antennae, their built-in, long-range communication devices that spread the news:

There were instructional broadcasts that informed

every insect within range exactly how to do it – how to stand-up! The little critters fell flat on their faces and mandibles in first attempts to get upright. But with some practice, balance was achieved. They organized. They seemed to actually get smarter, gain knowledge and intelligence and were more aware of the world around them. They were taller. The standing insects certainly acquired much more *confidence* than ever before in anything they worked on. The new perspective of the universe was responsible for the advanced *Change* the critters felt inside. It was as if the Insect Collective could do anything! INSECTS COULD BAND TOGETHER AND TAKE OVER THE WORLD!!

Insects marched. They raided houses, buildings and other human structures. The insect campaigns were not for food, they were for DOMINANCE. They were to control large areas of land and whatever was on the land. Different species of insects, some that were natural enemies, put aside their endless wars and joined forces! Intelligences greatly increased among insects, which no longer acted like dumb creatures. They strategized. They had a plan.

Ants were the prime movers of the rebellion, especially warrior-ants, the toughest and strongest of the species. Ants organized and designed the whole new reality of the "smart insect," where nothing was gathered for the Queen-ants. Ants were no longer drone-slaves that worked their whole lives in service to the ant-elites. There was no more insect royalty. The New Wave was truly a push for "Power to the Individual Insect" for the good of the collective. The Rebellion was a completely different way of viewing the universe. FREEDOM was the cry. *Change* from old ways was the New Way. The group mattered and not the former bug leaders. Ant Queens were killed!

The revolution also included millipedes and centipedes and a wide spectrum of flying insects. Even diets changed to plant-based, rather than traditional carnivore appetites.

Bees saw and tuned to the vibration of the vast Insect Collective. They also grew in intelligence and discarded old ways. New directives superseded what came before. Like ants, bees no longer served the Queens. They also revolted and *killed Queens!* **Chaos! Anarchy!** Tremendous numbers of drone and worker bees took and consumed massive reservoirs of pollen (power) for themselves! The lower classes now ruled the hives! Bees made it possible that all insects could have access to the treasures that were once exclusively given to Queens. But most important of all, bees planned the end of humanity!

Pillywog and Eppinefferin marched along a line of bugs to one of the new rebel rallies. Various kinds of insects in great numbers took over a human cabin in the woods. People vacated the premises when more than 100 trillion insects slowly marched inside the cabin at the same time. Millions of lightning bugs formed a big sign on the outer wall of the building, which directed the insects to the meeting place.

Pillywog told Eppinefferin, "I 'ear a bumble bee is the guest speaker tonight."

"Yeah, yeah. I 'eard that too, mate. I can't believe the bees 'ave control of our revolution now. We started the whole bloody rebellion, ya know? Remember? We're the ones *standing up*…for our rights, right? We were the first! Yeah, us cockroaches were the ones who started the whole fing. No one remembers that. *Bees. Freakin' bees.* Who likes bees? They're so loud, and I noticed…they're smug."

"They'll never give us roaches any credit, Eppi. But I like bees."

"What?"

"Be fair. I mean. Bees can fly an' all; we canna do that, mate. Be fair. Oh, you see what I did there? Be fair, ah, like in bee fair? Aye? Ha, ha." Pillywog said and laughed.

Eppinefferin replied, "Yeah, that was very funny, mate. Wonder what this *important* meeting is about, eh? 'Ave any ideas, Pilly?"

"Dunno. I fink they want us to fuck more and create more soldiers for freedom, for the collective. Wot 'bout you, wot you fink?"

"I say news from the fronts. Humans are spooked at our numbers and especially 'cos we're walking on two legs now. Yeah, they're on two legs and got incredible size on us. But we got the numbers! Big numbers, and we're organized. Gettin' smarter every day! Aye?"

"Yeah. Might be right, Pilly? It might be news we're winning the war and humans are scared of us, of what we might do next, aye?"

"Super. I'll bet the humans want to negotiate?"

"This is exciting. Look how many of us are at the rally."

The bugs entered the cabin and found a spot where they could stand together. All of the 6-leggers stood upright, in unison, proudly.

The place was filled to capacity. Floor, walls and ceiling were covered in all kinds of insects, insects on the same side and *together,* could change the world. The flyers and lightning bugs buzzed the air in wide swoops, circles and dives that really jazzed up the crowd. It was loud! It was the largest assembly of bugs Pilly and Eppi had ever seen! After the buzzes, cricks, creaks, and screeches were expressed, the meeting came to order. Movements were halted; everyone had their positions and listened carefully over their antennae.

There were plenty of bees in the crowd, but the one and only bumblebee, the guest speaker, was due to arrive soon. The insects were anxious to hear whatever the news (war plans) was or whatever information was presented before them. The bugs were *whooped up* to really fight: invade human homes! Sting and bite the fuck out of human skin! THEY WANTED WAR! They wanted blood, human blood! It was as if something unnatural consumed the 6-leggers. Missing from the Revolution were spiders. Arachnids, and all their varieties, were oddly not a part of the Great Insect Rebellion. Did the number of legs matter? Spiders thought a lot about this new business of war. They had no quarrel with people and wanted the status quo.

In buzzed the Bumblebee in that strange *ridged* pattern that was <u>not flying</u> and only shared by hummingbirds. (Their natural anti-gravity wave made bumblebees extremely cocky). Her name was Gertrude. The huge crowd flapped their wings, chirped, cricked, creaked and screeched, as fat/royal Gertrude landed on a special area centrally located.

Soon, the chatter and clatter, a sign of respect, ceased and the rally came to quiet order. The bugs heard Gertrude say:

"You all are waiting to hear news from the front,

which is precisely what I have to tell you. You all are waiting to attack, sharpening your full array of offensive skills. You await word from the bees, your commanders, when to MARCH, as you are ready to destroy the human race! Well, that's not going to happen! The war is over! Or, I should say, your part in the war is over! Do you hear me, comrades?! We are sure to win now…in our new approach…"

The massive crowd was not pleased. They were ready to fight and kill to the max! What the fuck? No battle? No battlefield? No glory? *Where's the fun in that?* They buzzed and chattered loud once again.

Some expressed: "Not good enough!" "Explain yourself!" "Why not fight?!" "We want to fight humans!" "It's our fight, too!" "Let us fight! Why can't we do our part in the war?!" "Why change tactics?"

Gertrude flapped her small wings, way too tiny for normal flight. "I will explain."

The crowd calmed down, eventually, and listened…

"We believe the spiders," said the bumblebee.

"Wot?"

"She said she believed the spiders."

"What the spiders say?"

"They're not a part of our rebellion. Fuckin' spiders!"

"They are smart, though."

"Hear me!" Getrude shouted. "Spiders are very intelligent and we found out why they're not with us in our great cause. Listen! They said, and it seems to be true: If we proceed as we originally planned with an all-out war, invade them directly…they will retaliate and bomb us with chemicals everywhere that will kill us, every one of us! Gas that will not harm them in the least.

This will happen if we proceed overtly. They'll kill all of us! Do you understand?!"

One of the bees said to the bumblebee: "They will never kill us bees! They know not to do that because we're needed for cross-pollination. Their whole crop industry would collapse without us!"

"Brother," Gertrude said. "That's why they keep you honey bees in special *hives*. Of course, bees are essential for life. They don't keep other insects in special homes. They build bee homes and they care for us. They need us for honey; we are necessary. Hives are safe."

"I don't fink this is much of a revolution, Gertie." Pillywog tossed in his two cents. I mean, you're *not* going to massacre the humans? Wot? I don't understand."

"Insects! Bugs! Hear me! I did not finish the news! What we are going to do is *hurt* the humans…"

"Wot's that?!"

"What are you gonna do?!"

Gertrude informed the masses just as other bumbles informed their troops at the same time: "Top bees in the war-effort have decided and have come to a drastic decision. We are going to cross our legs and not pollinate for one season, for the greater good. Yes, both sides will take heavy losses for a time. But it won't be the end of the world and possibly, possibly, in time…our message will get through? We won't be gas-bombed from the skies and be virtually wiped out, see? Our numbers will remain at acceptable levels this way…"

"That's a big relief."

"Thank the spiders."

3 The Aurora is God

"IF only it was true! God! You spoke to me in dreams! But today, in the awake world of the living, you've come to me and now you really SPEAK to me!" Jannik Sommerstrom was a wild-man, a renegade to his normal and very conservative Norwegian family in Oslo. Every last member of his family believed Jannik was "crazy." Let's flashback to a previous moment in time…

Years ago, in 2015, on his way home from the Bended Way pub in Oslo, an incredible FEELING overwhelmed the man. Everything around young Mr. Sommerstom appeared somewhat different to his eyes and in his mind. It was not the Stella Artois 'talking.' He was not that drunk. He had walked the walk from the pub to his home a hundred times. His steps were sure and he was lucid, had all of his faculties. *What was this new sensation that everything around me seems a bit different, somehow changed?*

Jannik remembered that Gruber's department store windows were always trimmed in red. Suddenly, they were painted in green? Odd. It would have been a large task and taken much time to complete such a painting project on 16 floors. And Jannik remembered that he saw the red trim only a day ago.

Then, there was the Norwegian flag. Between the Bended Way pub and his house, there were two displays of the national flag. When he got closer, the man noticed a strange color on the flag that was never there before. "What? Dark blue? Navy blue? No, no. That's not right." In Jannik's mind, and as far as he remembered, the dark cross on the Norwegian flag was always black! Black! Black, white and red were the colors of Norway's flag, *not white, red and dark blue?* Mister Sommerstrom wondered about the apparent color change of the flag and the color change of the department store windows. He said aloud, "Have I gone color-blind? Certain colors are different to me now? I don't know."

JS decided to check the flag when he came to it a second time. Possibly, that one outdoor flag had faded and wasn't black anymore? But when he saw the next flag on the way home, it also contained a dark blue cross and the flag appeared new.

It was the 3rd weirdness or *memory-change* that shattered Jannik inside, slightly, and he doubted the very world he'd always known. On the corner of Cabrea and Dunsdorff, stood an 8-foot statue of Norway's greatest war hero, Gunnar Sonsteby. A plaque in the stone base was well-known to him and also about every native in town:

"Gunner Sonseby (1918-2012) – Norway's greatest

war hero, a leader in the Resistance Movement during World War II, known for his daring sabotage operations and his many prestigious decorations, which include the 3 Swords War Cross. Statue given to the city of Oslo by the University of Edinburgh."

Jannik didn't usually read the words on the plaque that he'd seen many times over, but he read them this evening…and the young man was *absolutely astounded.* Right on the heels of the color-changes that made him think he went color-blind, now the famous words etched in the plaque appeared different to him? Where was the "t" in Sonsteby? And the plaque never misspelled the university's name before. Edinborough was now spelled Edinburgh? *What?! That's wrong and it was never wrong before! Am I going out of my mind? Has anyone else seen this? Why haven't they corrected…no, it was right before! Was it changed?"*

Weeks went by and Jannik Sommerstom was virtually disowned by his family. He ranted for days and days about what he remembered and the bizarre changes that had strangely occurred. He desperately wanted his family to understand and remember what he remembered. Not one of them agreed. Not one saw an Old World that was snatched away like the 'Body-Snatchers' and replaced by something different. According to the other Sommerstroms: everything today was exactly the way it has always been. There had been no odd changes. He found that everyone, including neighbors, felt the same way. He left.

Jannik left with money that he had in his savings and traveled to New Zealand. He was motivated by a weird idea. He had been there before. Jannik remembered that

New Zealand was *one island;* he was sure of it. But when he examined the world map, he noticed NZ was in two pieces? There was a "North" and "South" island now, although the country was basically horizontal. In Mr. Sommerstom's mind, it once looked like a worm with two antennas. One worm. But now, New Zealand appeared like a worm cut in two pieces.

Jannik's plan was to *blow his mind* by taking a boat through Cook's Strait (waterway that separates North and South islands) and see what happened? What thoughts come to mind? How creepy would it be to travel the waterway that Jannik knew *did not exist a year ago?*

That's just what we did: He joined a New Zealand tour-boat that regularly made trips up, down and through Cook's Strait, the waterway between islands. It was very creepy to Jannik. The weather was dreary, misty, almost rain. He absolutely was positive of his memories…

Jannik had visited the town of Cook once before! It wasn't a strip of water; it was a town! Towns were often named after British sea captains. Nelson was a seaport town not far away. And Cook, after Captain Cook, was a landlocked town! He was there! *He drank in a pub in the town of Cook!* He remembered the music and the waitresses. The man checked maps and…the town no longer existed. Today, Jannik Sommerstrom was called 'crazy,' and there were two parts to New Zealand.

When he returned home, he discovered another glaring oddity that he knew never existed before: Svalbard. Svalbard?? Who the hell ever heard of Svalbard? And yet, when he asked around, it seemed as if everyone had heard of Svalbard Island except for him! *What? Can't be. But again, it's happening to me!* A small island north of Norway belongs to Norway and is in the Guinness Book of Records as the most northerly inhabited village with a Post Office. Jannik knew what the record was formerly; it was a small village at the tip of north Alaska, not a Norwegian mailing address. "What world am I in?!" Jannik screamed. "Am I going crazy? Must be! How can my vivid memories be so wrong?! Why God? Won't you speak to me and help me out of my pain? I have to know…*what is wrong with me!!??*"

Later, the broken-to-the-core man made a final trip…

He took the last of his money, bought a lot of supplies and exiled himself from the world. Everywhere he went, he saw signs of a new reality that had replaced the old one. Not everywhere, but here and there, and also in some product names. He noticed: The Dollar Tree was now The Dollar Store, even with the same green and white colors. He remembered Jiffy Peanut Butter, but now he found it was *always JIF?* There was a Pollo Loco stand in his hometown, but now it changed to *El Pollo Loco,* which was not what he remembered. Jannik wanted to end his life over these micro details. The disparity between what was and what is now made him *permanently move to Svalbard Island,* more north, where it was even colder and very inhospitable. He lived in a small shack that suited his needs.

"This island was never here before! My whole life, I would have seen it on maps. *It was never there!* Now, I'm sitting on it, ha! And what of my dreams? Dreams where a Voice of God speaks from the sky?! God is the Aurora?? Well, I haven't seen the Borealis in months, although it's due and I'm more likely to see it now that…"

Suddenly, a loud Voice was heard outside his shack: **"Jannik!"**

The young man immediately *ran outside* and the bright, magical, overwhelming lights caught his eye. Like his dreams…God was here.

"You are not insane, my friend. You are awake, you are aware, you can see where others cannot! The planet has been unnaturally changed and there are only a few, special people who realize this. You are special, Jannik. You are right; they are blind. Now go out into the world with a confidence, with a belief in yourself that you have never known before. Fly free, my friend."

4 Pandragon of Prague

IF only we could speak to dragons.

The beast was called the *Pandragon of Prague,* but his real name was a secret ["Phlozoraan"]. It was the end of the year 1599. As far as anyone knew, the Pandragon was the last of his kind. Legends and passed on stories, in all parts of Europe, were filled with dragons and "flying demons" that breathed and exhaled great plumes of fire. Thousands of dragons of incredible proportions once flew in the skies of the Old World, and accounted for the stories and distant memories in people. Now, there was only one and he made his lair atop Mount Snezka, the highest peak in the territory.

The Pandragon enjoyed his flights over the capital of Prague because of the high number of people in the city. The beast swooped in and continuously *blasted roars* hundreds of times louder than a lion's roar! The sounds overhead terrified the simple people below. He loved it when they scattered and ran for shelter in buildings. Often, the Pandragon landed on rooftops, breathed fire and *torched* a few of the wooden structures in town. The damage was minimal and human beings seemed to have been spared the full Pandragon's wrath.

Prague's citizens were wrapped in fear. "Because the beast hasn't killed anyone we know of, that doesn't mean it won't in future!" "What does it want? Stories tell us you can talk to dragons if you are in their favor. Has anyone tried signs or signals or simply *shouting* at it?" "Maybe it wants food? We should put out piles of food." "Maybe it wants love and understanding? One of our brave youths should try to attract it to its favorite rooftop, the great library, and talk to the beast." "That's from an old man; why don't *you* climb up on the library's roof and talk some sense into the beast?" "Ha, ha, ha." "Ha!"

That was the scene and situation in the capital city at the end of 1599. A "Pandragon" flew down from the mountain peak on occasion and semi-terrorized townsfolk, set some fires and then returned back home up to his high lair. With the coming new century, people wanted a *change* from years of the Pandragon's intimidation and frightening demeanor when it invaded the city...

The people flocked to the city's churches for answers, as if religious leaders could somehow exorcise the flying demon as they have with a few possessed individuals. Could Prague be cleared or cleansed by the priests? One sect of the priesthood was well-schooled in old scrolls, books and sacred parchments. The zealots discovered a recently-translated prophecy, which read:

The last dragon will end its reign when two brave souls seek its words, not in vain.

The prime zealot interpreted the new passage to mean: <u>Two of the townsfolk must climb Mount Snezka and attempt to speak with the Pandragon.</u> The motion was carried by the Burgermeister and two "volunteers" were quickly chosen. The selection seemed obvious. The bravest heroes in the Anglo-Spanish War (1595) were Salvador Steflic and Walter Jirak. They served together on the war council and were strong, young men who now served the State as well as the military.

As expected, Steflic and Jirak did not hesitate and accepted the mission without the smallest objection. They laughed, drank and believed they might get to talk to the infamous Pandragon, the tormentor of Prague. Both believed their lives were charmed. On the battlefield, they prevailed as lucky survivors. Why not be heroes again and prevail over the great, flying beast? - was their thought process.

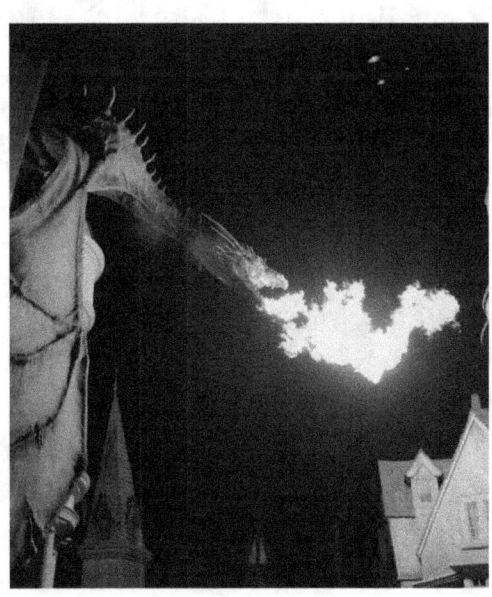

That night, the Pandragon once again flew down from its lair and landed on the great library's roof. The sound of his roar was incredibly loud. Walter and Salvador got their first good and very terrifying look at the beast. The Pandragon burned and singed the roof across the way, which was used to being burned and singed by the beast. Not a soul was seen in the streets of Prague, near the library. The young men viewed the fiery spectacle between shutters of a large window. The fire bell alarm was sounded.

The beast seemed awfully angry…at something.

Walter said to Sal, "I wonder what he's so pissed at? Aye?"

"Yeah, and yet 'e's not burning the city to ashes. You know damn well the creature could, easily. But 'e doesn't, eh? Curious. Does 'e just want a little attention? Ha, love and understanding? Maybe 'e's in pain and only wants to cry out in the night?"

Walter expressed, "I wonder if we'll get to talk to 'im, or, or, 'e swallows us whole, eh? Ha, ha. Wot you think, my friend?"

"Ha, ha." Salvador laughed, pulled on his beard, smiled, then said, "We live many lives, Walter. Why not risk one on supreme adventure, aye?"

"Supreme adventure. I like that. Tomorrow, early before dawn, we'll get our gear and make the climb. We'll be fine. Wot stories we'll tell, right? The girls will love it. No?" Walter's eyes sparkled.

Both looked again at the beast as another fire-force was expelled from his mouth and into the night's sky. Their expressions changed from naïve wonder to concern. With the loudest roar of them all that shook the building, their faces turned to worry. *Tomorrow, were they going to throw their lives away?*

Tomorrow came and the young men were packed and ready to go. Backpacks, climbing gear, food, warm clothes, boots and much courage in their hearts. Snezka was actually an "easy climb" to real mountain climbers. Passed the Bohemian Forest, its incline was not very steep. There were steep patches where equipment was needed. All in all, the ascent was mostly a rough and tedious walk uphill.

It was nearly at the halfway point in the climb that the boys heard a flutter in the air. They hung onto a ledge that stood on the side of a gigantic boulder. They heard the sound again, this time: *louder!* It was Dragon Sign! *The big, bloody beast suddenly swooped down from above and opened its massive mouth, and...*

Breathed out a jet of FIRE and it torched the trees and brush right alongside them! The stream created a vertical wall of flames only a few feet from Walter and Salvador. The boys were on a canyon-like precipice without being tied to ropes and *Sal lost his footing and fell!*

Before he crashed down 80 feet upon rocks...

The Pandragon saved his life! The beast flew down farther, extended his right wing and caught Salvador Steflic. His fall was broken and the young man balanced on the jagged wing. In midair, the Pandragon moved his wing so Sal hopped on the beast's body. Then, the beast flew up to where Walter was on the ledge and extended his left wing out to him. Walt knew to get on and he joined his friend on the body of the creature.

The Pandragon roared words in a language the boys understood. The beast yelled, **"Now, hold on for dear**

life!!"

They flew up, higher and higher, with every flap of the dragon's enormous wings. Walter and Salvador were secure in the jagged furrows of the beast. They held on tight to the irregular exterior. They flew over the wall of fire, up and up. They looked into each other's eyes, which had tears of excitement: *They rode a dragon!* The boys felt pure exhilaration! It was heavenly. They felt: No Fear. The feeling was that the creature wasn't a danger and wasn't going to hurt them.

The beast turned his head and looked back at them and laughed: **"Ha, ha, ha, haaaa!"**

In a minute, they reached the top of Mount Snezka and found megalithic ruins from prehistory. Obviously, this was the Pandragon's lair and no one known had ever seen these ruins and lived to tell the tale.

Later, after they dismounted and were given the "cook's tour" of the place, the two gentlemen and Pandragon got settled on rocks and held a round of questions:

"Call me: Phlo...although, no one is supposed to know that."

"Flo?"

"Not Flo as in Florence. Phlo! Phlo, as in Phlozoraan..."

"Oooh. Wow. Phlozoraan. That's a neat name," Walter said.

"You have an amazing home here." The view was incredible and the cool winds increased. Salvador expressed, "We are extraordinarily fortunate to be here and for you, Phlo, to share your home with us. But I want to be very clear? Do you have any intentions on, on…?"

"No sir, ha. I am not going to *eat* you. We dragons have a third eye you do not see. It is a total panorama of realization and understanding. I know what you are going to say before you say it because I see the light that is in your hearts. You do not think I would speak to just anyone who climbed my mountain, do you?"

"You wouldn't?" Sal asked.

"No. You two are from prophecy. Chroniclers. Recorders of history, or events, I should say. You have even steered history, yes? You are here to hear my story and retell it to your people."

"We can do that." Walter smiled.

Salvador also smiled and nodded. "Yes. Happy to do that."

"Get comfortable, as I tell you what happened long ago and why I must leave soon."

"You are known as the *Last Dragon,* Phlozoraan. Are you saying you are going to die soon?" Salvador innocently asked.

"Ah, no, not at all. A ship is coming to take me back home…"

"Really? A ship? Back where? Where do you come from?" The boys were stunned and curious.

"Ha, ha," Phlo laughed. **"No, it is not a ship that sails the 7 seas. We come from space, a place that circles one of the stars in the night's sky. I often cry to go home and I will be there soon."**

"Why are you leaving, Phlo?" Sal asked, sadly.

"That is very personal, Salvador. Let me tell my story."

"Of course."

"We dragons originally came from a massive

planet going around the orange-giant star you call 'Betelgeuse.' Our planet's name is Dragonwyck. We colonized your Earth long ago and warred with a Reptilian species, who believed they owned your planet and everything on it because of an early claim. With technology on the intelligent, two-legged Lizard's side, the War raged on with no clear winner. A resolution, truce, treaty had to be negotiated, especially since the emergence of millions of human beings. The settlement was: The Reptilians won their claim, but would rule the planet from the shadows (unseen), while thousands of dragons had to leave Earth...all except for one. Only I was allowed to remain, the last of my kind. But I hold vast memories of wondrous days long ago, and I swear, my new friends...my mind and heart also hold the spirits of my brothers and sisters, long gone. My kind drives starships and freely roams the fantastic, cosmic universe. I was abandoned here, and must stay as the last one, as prophecy decreed, or as per the Agreement..."

Salvador interrupted Phlozoraan, "Wait, Phlo, I'm confused. You said a ship from space is coming to take you back? So, you *are* leaving us?"

"I explained to you how things were for ages. But recently, when I saw a new atrocity that will happen in the city of Rome, this was shown to my kind through transmission and through my prayer...for them to please END what I consider a *Prison Sentence* for me and not fulfilling a Prophecy – end my reign here over Snezka, the Bohemian Forest and the city of Prague. Please. And, gentlemen, I am the happiest dragon in all of Dragonwyck because they have answered my prayers! Positively! Last night, my assault on Prague from the library's roof was my plea to be free...*and I will be!* A ship is coming very soon, my friends. I am so pleased." Phlozoraan smiled a big toothy smile.

"I am happy for you, Phlo, former Pandragon of Prague!"

"Walter, Sal, did you notice I never killed one person? I was all bark and no bite, aye?"

"You came close to us on the rock ledge," Salvador said with a smile.

"Ah! I shoot with precision. If I wanted to have struck you, I would have. Ha. The townsfolk needed to rebuild a lot of those old structures I burned down, anyway. Hell, I put them to work. It was good for the State's economy, ha."

"That's one way to look at it, Phlo," Walter commented.

"I have a serious question for the great Dragon of Prague. I don't know if you will answer the question, my giant friend..." Salvador Steflic brought the light, cheerful mood down. He had a point and wondered if Phlozoraan would go for it: "For us to be real reporters and remember the truth of who you really are and what happened before..."

"Yes?"

"I was simply wondering...if...if..."

"IF?"

"I mean for the report! You see, people will want to know the whole story; *why are you really leaving?* I know you said it was very personal to you. *If* you would tell us this tragedy, a 'new atrocity' that will soon happen in the future, in Rome? Would you mind telling us?"

Phlo burped Fire as an immediate reaction, and it scared the boys.

"Sorry, sorry. That was some gas that ignited. No worries."

Sal said, "If you are not comfortable with revealing…?"

"No, no. It is just very sad what will transpire in Rome's 'Campo de' Fiori,' they will call it in the years to come. I made my kind see the horrible wars and this final event in Rome was the *last straw.* A revolutionary, an astronomer and beautiful theorist was right. He wrote books and spoke out against the Church. He denied core Catholic doctrines. And because he spoke and spread the Truth, *he was killed!* But the way he was killed was an ultimate disgrace. Children were brought into the courtyard to witness the event. They were told: This is what will happen to you if you disobey the Catholic Church of Rome and the Throne of England. Giordana Bruno was *burned at the stake.* Fire will destroy the man…in the next hour. Fire. Fire, of all things! Ugh.." Tears flowed from Phlo's big eyes.

Walter and Salvador wanted very much to ease his pain. They concocted an idea that might help the big beast.

"Remember! Your kind are coming for you! Your prison sentence is over and you'll be home on Dragonwyck…with all your friends."

"I know what you should do, Phlo! Take one more swipe at Prague, aye? Maybe the other end of the library's roof? For old time's sake. Go ahead! Enjoy yourself. They need the work! It's fine. For the last time, you know? Before the ship comes to take you away.

Yes?"

   "Yes! I think I will."

5 Noseferatu

IF the leading expert on vampirism was much more than that.

The troupe called the 'Royal Filmmakers of London' landed in Prague, Czechoslovakia, with the intentions of filming the infamous Count Orlav. So much dark and devious publicity circulated around the count whose home was Castle Revelle on top of Mount Snezka. It was well-known throughout Europe that Orlav was the leading expert on vampires and vampirism. Rumors persisted among citizens of Prague that the *count was a real vampire*. Local police had considered that Orlav could be a vampire and authorities fully inspected Castle Revelle. There were missing people who strangely disappeared from the area, but nothing was ever found that implicated the count.

Orlav was a sinister-looking character in appearance. He was on the small-side, bald, rat-ish, had white skin and always dressed in black. His fingers were long and also his nails. It seemed as if the count had fangs, although no one was quite sure. Orlav had a very big nose that covered most of his mouth. The authorities concluded that the man who appeared as a vampire, was not one. He was, in reality, just some very old expert on vampirism and had been obsessed with them and studied their history all of his ancient life. He "dressed the part" and was actually *a kind soul underneath a gruesome exterior?*

Town officials did little to dispel rumors of Orlav's nefarious dealings. What exactly did he do in his laboratory with all the strange, electrical equipment? His answer to officials was always: "Scientific Experimentation." Speculation ran amok among townsfolk that the count drained people of their blood. So far, they never stormed the castle, although many drunk citizens desired to. Truth was: Villagers on the outskirts of the Bohemian Forest were far too scared to ever scale the peak and mount an attack on Orlav.

The film troupe from London, which consisted of twelve male members and a single woman, stopped at the Blue Boar Inn at the foot of Mount Snezka…and asked for confirmation…

"The castle at the top of the peak, that is Count Orlav's castle, is it not, sir?" Linus Strather, director, asked the hefty barman. His group entered the Inn and sat down after their long ride in two carriages with horses.

"That be where the monster lives, sir," the man coldly replied.

"You said…monster? I thought the law cleared Orlav from any wrongdoings?"

"That be true, sir. The royal seal doesn't make him not a monster, now, aye? I've answered your question. Answer me this: What business does your people have with the count?" There was no tension in the bar. The barman had a smile on his face. He was curious and appreciated the sudden profit to his register. Soon, his two daughters brought drinks to the troupe and took their orders.

"We're from London and we're here to make a film. Vampires are all the rage in social circles of the court. It was werewolves and lycanthropy, but now, I'm afraid it's back to blood-suckers…"

"Sir." The man poured a hard ale for Linus. "Vampiria and lycans are not jokes 'round these parts. People have really disappeared, mysteriously…"

"You know of this, truly?" Strather asked, sincerely.

"It be true, and more than that: Dead bodies 'ave been found over the years, completely drained of blood, sir. Our doctor will confirm the fact of bloodless corpses. Yes, sir. So, wot are we ta think?"

By this time, two friends of the director (producers of the film) joined him. They heard the last part of the conversation.

"This is more of my troupe, Alex and Lemuel."

"Glad to meet you, sirs. I'll 'ave drinks for you in a second. Me name's Shamus."

"Nice place you have here, Shamus."

Alex asked, "How's the road? Uphill? Two carriages, will they make the journey to the castle?"

Shamus responded as he set ales down on the bar: "The police made it up with no problems. If you have four strong horses…?"

"We do," Linus answered.

"Then, you'll make the castle. But I warn you fine, gentlemen. Don't go. Turn back now. That is…if you value your lives, sirs?"

"Why?" the director asked, seriously.

The barkeep said, "The police and officials were a bloody army, but wot you 'ave 'ere? A dozen thin blokes from England and a woman? I'd say: keep your guns in your hands and watch your backs at all times, gentlemen."

Strather expressed, "We will be careful, my good man." Linus smiled, dismissed the warning and considered it part of the local color or rumor mill. Then, he shouted, "A round of drinks for one and all!"

Ten villagers in the Inn *cheered*. "Yay!" "Make mine a double."

Lemuel turned to Alex and Linus, smiled and said, "Bottoms' up. Tomorrow, we die. Ha!"

"It was a lark while it lasted, eh?" He *clinked* glasses with Linus and Lemuel. More laughs.

The director said to the two producers, "Orlav is probably, ah, probably *not* a vampire. But, but…I think we all should wear the holy cross? Wotcha think?"

Alex replied, "I'll make sure we have them under our clothes…"

"Good."

Much later, the horses and carriages made the trek up the hill. The troupe entered through a large door that was already opened. They encountered a sign, ink on paper, left in the dark entryway. It read: *Find rooms to your liking. All accommodations have been prepared. My routine is never coming out during the day. I will appear around the dinner table long after sunset. My servant, Dwight, will see to your needs and show you around my home. Welcome."*

Later, the group gathered around the table and Dwight served dinner. Dwight was an odd character: A small man who walked funny because of a twisted back that appeared to have a very large, round indentation. He told them, "The Master won't be eating. Enjoy. He does not consume this type of food, you see? Go right ahead." The food was good and impressed the people from London.

Alex said to Linus, "What do you think will happen when Orlav discovers we're not out to make a documentary on vampires and this is not an elaborate interview, but we're making a fictional movie and the main star is a vampire?"

"You mean what's he going to think when he finds out we want him in the lead role? I mean, who else in the world could play the part better, aye?"

"Yeah."

"I suspect we'll see if he ever had any Hollywood aspirations, eh? Can you imagine Orlav at the Oscars?"

"Ha, ha, ha, ha!"

Felicity Langer (star of British stage and screen), the one lady in the film, walked to Linus and Alex. "What are you boys laughing at?"

"Are you really going to let the count bite your neck, Felicity?"

"Ha, ha. It says it in the script so, I guess, I have no choice, eh?" The threesome all lit up cigarettes.

"Well. Don't let his nose get in the way. Ha, ha." A few of the others heard what Linus said and also laughed. "Ha, ha."

"Good evening!" the count shouted as he jumped out from behind black curtains. Everyone in the room jumped in complete surprise and Felicity screamed!

Orlav laughed. "Ha, ha! I meant nothing by it, gentlemen and sweet lady. Only, ah, something to get your blood pumping, oui?"

"Yes, yes. Ha, ha. Funny."

"I see, Count Orlav. Something to break the ice, yes, of course."

"Good people, I must tell you: I have ears like a *bat!* I've heard every word. I understand you want me to play the lead role of Count Rammstein. I agree with what you said, mister director: Who better to play the part of a vampire than ME! Me, me! Ha!" Orlav was a twisted, wretched creature. Was he real? Or, was his life an act?

"Then, you'll do it, Count?" Linus asked.

"Of course!" Orlav yelled with glee.

Everyone celebrated, drank and shook his cold/cold hand.

There was not a peep during the night. Most of the troupe were convinced strange things would occur in the night and they did not. The quiet night calmed their nerves and they collectively relaxed and went about business. In the day, the film crew got everything ready for the night shoot. All the shoots would be conducted at night.

"He really gives the impression that he's a vampire, doesn't he?" Linus Strather expressed to Lemuel.

"Are we sure he is not?"

"Lem, look how quickly he jumped at acting in the film. Of course, it's all an act."

Then, everything was ready and it was time to shoot the first scene: *Count Rammstein welcomes Carlos, future servant to the Count and insect-eater, into his castle.* Everyone was in their positions, the technicians and the actors, producers and director.

Did Count Orlav appear out of nothing? The background was black and it was hard to tell. He stood perfectly still on his mark and looked hideous. No makeup; he was his normal self.

"Cue Carlos. Have him enter and…"

"No, no, we're not going to do that," Orlav interrupted the director. He showed his real fangs and hypnotized the whole group around him. He forced the cameraman to work the camera. "Film!" he screamed. The people kept in stationary positions while he literally *flew from one of their necks to the other!* Each person dropped to the floor with less blood in their bodies. A bloody, bloody hour passed as he gorged on Felicity as his 10th and last victim. All the while, the cameraman and Linus watched in sheer horror! Orlav made the film he wanted to make and approached Linus Strather for one more kill.

Linus thought very fast and opened up a large bag of cocaine he'd saved for the Wrap Party. He broke it out and showed Orlav how to snort the powder up his big, fucking nose! He'd never indulged in coke. The drug was such a potent provider of pleasure for the old vampire, he spared the lives of Linus and the cameraman.

"Can you get me more of this?" SNIFF.

"Yes, we can."

6 The Family Curse

What IF the world was a world of werewolves? Everyone was a wolfman or a wolfwoman. What might happen in a society of strong beasts with big jaws, teeth, fangs and a lot of hair over their bodies?

Don't get the wrong idea. On the planetoid known as Dragos, the werewolves were sophisticated, cultured, and they *spoke*. They used many of the same conveniences that humans have created and used.

Our story begins one evening inside the lovely castle-home of Blake and Emily Romanoff in the misty mountains of Gamorra. It was a very special occasion with a "guest of honor" for dinner: Their young son, Targ, brought home his fiancé, Flem, to meet his parents.

The boy beast was excited and nervous. His sudden

fiancé was also very nervous. She loved Targ and desperately hoped she'd make a good impression on his well-known parents. She wore a smattering of clothing that was stunning. Her lashes were extended and her long nails were immaculately painted.

The initial meeting and small chat went well and the whole family, which included Uncle Shite, Auntie M and also little Zimo, soon sat down at the dinner table.

Lycans [lesser werewolves] brought out the first appetizer, which was the most delicious rat soup anyone's ever tasted, and served each of the 7 places around the table. In minutes, the soup was followed by a splendid stuffed boar and a few rabbits on the side.

So far, Targ and Flem were supremely pleased at the first meeting. The Romanoff parents kept one eye on the girl. Yes, she appeared to be the perfect companion for Targ. But the night was young. Will she pass the big test that will occur in the next hour?

Loud, snarling sounds were heard throughout an exquisite dinner. Teeth and fangs tore into the hog's flesh and claws clutched old, sculpted goblets and glasses. The Romanoffs and special guest gorged themselves on the meat and washed it down with quarts of blood.

Lycan servants placed more assortments of meat on the wooden table in the monolithic castle that was once owned by the real (human) Romanoff family. This was during prehistoric times, before the werewolves controlled the world. Today, 2-legged wolves utilized all possessions that were once owned by their vampire masters. Vampire counts, countesses, barons, baronesses and other royalty had become extinct, killed by their hairy slaves on the very bleak planetoid with a small purple sun known as Dragos.

The Wolf Clan, once tortured slaves, now ruled a world that they inherited. Long ago, wolfmen and wolfwomen had constructed the castles and cared for the coffins. But now, they were the kings and queens and possessed the castles. Humans had not walked the dark surface of Dragos in 100 years. The first generation of freed werewolves also assumed the names of their former masters, while the next generation of beasts chose their own names.

Final growls and dinner digestion sounds died down to soft whispers of satisfaction. By candlelight, the lycans heaped even more meats and side-dishes on the table.

"Would you like more pink meat or the not so pink meat, dear?" Lady Romanoff asked of her son's fiancé.

The attractive she-wolf answered, "I am full. No, wouldn't think of it, M'Lady. My, it was a fine meal…"

"Oh, c'mon," replied the older wolfwoman. Lady Emily presided over the surprise dinner while the lycans prepared the food. "This was short notice…" She looked at her husband, Blake.

The old wolfman smiled and nodded. He looked at Targ with wrinkled approval on his hairy face and smiled.

The young werewolf beamed with happiness. The boy shouted, "More drinks, father! Let's celebrate my union with the beautiful Lady Flem! To our future and things to come!"

"Here, here!"

"I'll drink to that!"

"Not you, Zimo."

"Ha, ha!"

Blake and Emily drank and celebrated, but it was only a "show" for their son and his fiancé. This very thing had happened before, a few times. Targ was one amorous beastie and very popular with the ladies. But, in the past, right after dinner, the Moon rose and the test was on! Each young lady that was let in on **The Family Secret**, could not accept the truth, and *ran out of the castle in hysterics!* Will tonight be different? Will Targ ever find the happiness he deserves? Blake and Emily were hopeful and put on a happy face for the young ones, but they were very concerned. What will happen in about 20 minutes?

His wife continued, "…We prepared what we could with this, ah…brilliant news." She looked at the couple; they seemed much in love. "…Sudden engagement, although it seems like great news, yes?"

Blake assured them, "Believe me, you two. We are both very happy for you. You'll make a fine couple of Romanoffs." The patriarch waved his pipe with glee. "Beautiful girl, son. You sure know how to pick 'm."

"Thanks, dad. You'll love Flem."

The young she-Wolf batted her long, pretty lashes and showed more of her fangs in a big smile. "You're sweet," Flem responded. Then, she turned to Blake. "You're very knowledgeable, sir. Do you mind a few questions on what really happened years ago? I have parents that aren't too sure what happened in the old days."

Emily commented to her son, "Oh, she's a keeper, Targ. Curious one."

"By all means, my dear," Mr. Romanoff answered.

"Many legends have circulated over the ages." Targ added, "I tried to tell her that your stories are true, dad. But she didn't believe me."

"She didn't? Ha." The he-Wolf inhaled smoke from his pipe again. Then he checked the time as a giant hourglass in the corner nearly emptied its top portion.

Emily smiled and stated, "We'll have to convince dear Flem of a few things, tonight. She appears…open-minded." The matriarch's face hid a multitude of secrets.

Flem finished her goblet of fresh blood and stated, "Yes, there's many conflicting stories, exaggerations and contradictions about the war…"

"You mean the war against vampires?" Blake quickly interjected.

"Yes, sir."

"Ha." Mrs. Romanoff laughed. "No, no, my dear. It wasn't a *war* with our masters."

Blake looked at his son. Targ shrugged.

"You're a respected authority, sir. You mean what your son told me is true?" the Wolf-girl asked, extremely interested in the real history of Dragos.

Emily also finished her goblet and said, "Absolutely."

Blake declared, "Well, Flem. If he told you one brave and daring Wolf, who later took his master's name of Lord Rothschild, convinced the other Wolfs to revolt, then that particular story is the truth."

The wild, hairy girl with razor-sharp claws still could not believe it. "But there was no battle, no bloody fields, no combat with vampires? No massacre for the glory of our race?!"

The Romanoffs laughed again. Now Emily checked the time. She looked at her family and newest member intently and was worried: *Would the love of her son's life be so understanding when she learned more in a matter of minutes?*

Blake coaxed Targ to state exactly what he informed his fiancé.

Targ said sincerely, "I told her what you told me, dad. You were there. You were one of them…"

"Who did what?" the father asked the boy.

"You, along with each Wolfen slave, decided to act as one after your 'Lord Rothschild' realized how you all could easily be freed. You dragged, everyone in unison, dragged your master's and lady's coffins out into the fields during Dragos' one hour of pure sunlight. That's what I told her. Then…you opened the lids."

"Did you also tell her what the Wolves did right after they opened the coffin lids, son?"

"No, what?" the girl asked with big eyes and long teeth.

Lady Emily laughed and told her the truth. "Ha, ha. The boys RAN like the frightened animals they were! Ha! Ah, ha."

She made the others laugh as well.

"Really? Ha, ha. Some war massacre." Flem was

amazed at the truth. "You simply, opened lids? Ha, ha. Outrageous."

"I didn't know that," Targ confessed. "Though, I can imagine your fears, dad. You were under vampire's spell for centuries. Heard 'bout what you guys found later, the charred/burned out remains."

Blake was a bit miffed, but hid it. He inquired, "Anything more you'd like to ask, dear?" He glanced at the time.

Emily understood what was contained within her husband's glance.

Flem stared at the last lycan servant that left the room.

Blake read her mind. "I know what you're going to ask. How can we former slaves of vampires now make slaves of the lycans?" Blake comfortably blew a smoke ring.

"Yes, exactly. By the way, I like the cute, floppy ears on your server, tonight."

"Ha." Blake answered her deep question: "Maybe it's natural, to be on the other end of the stick? You and your generation are right, Flem. It isn't right. Maybe in time, your generation will correct the flaws in ourselves?"

"Let's hope for the best," Emily agreed and her wrinkled, hairy face formed a wide smile.

Mr. Romanoff continued, "Funny thing is: lycans, our offspring with big dogs, eh? They want to serve us. They are loyal to the core and find pleasure or great purpose in serving us, a higher-class of creature, I must say. They're not oppressed, abused workers or slaves. We accept the lycan-dogs' services and care for them with respect and dignity."

Flem thought more about it. She was a thoughtful Wolf. "Still not right. Maybe some short day on Dragos, they'll lead a revolution against their masters?"

"Good one, Flem." Blake applauded the girl. "I really like her, Targ. She has spunk, and I like spunk in a girl."

Emily burst with pride as she faced her son. But then her expression soon changed to fear as she once again spied the hourglass. She glared into Blake's eyes. The Moon was ready to rise.

"Mother and I will retire to the sitting room. You kids can join us in a moment." Blake casually smiled as if tonight was any normal evening on Dragos. It wasn't. He hid his concern. He and wife stood up nervously, shook a little and left the dark and dusty room.

Flem organized the plates and wanted to be useful.

Targ stopped her with, "Leave it, please. Rawlph will clean up the mess. He loves it."

Her strong claws dropped the dishes and nearly cracked them. "Whoops." She smiled.

He held her tight.

They passionately kissed a big and hairy kiss. He stroked her fur. Then she broke the affectionate mood and loving embrace with a brilliant thought. "A little bat told me there's a few things your family's been hiding."

"Why do you say that, love?" Targ asked, now the curious and nervous one.

Flem pointed firmly at the hourglass in the corner. "Never seen a glass that big. In less than a minute, all the sand will be at the bottom. Something's going to happen, right? They kept looking at it."

Targ knew his fiancé was one intelligent Wolf. Here goes… "We…how do I say it?"

Her big hands were placed on her wide hips. "Say it!"

"We have a family secret…"

Flem was intrigued. "Which is?"

"In a m-minute you'll see for yourself." Targ suddenly shook and could not control one arm.

"Lord! Targ, are you Okay? Are you sick or something? What's going to happen?" There was fear in Flem's powerful, brown eyes.

He held her and she also shook. "Do you love me?" he asked her very seriously.

"Yes!"

"Then trust me now." Targ *changed.* In great pain, he growled and dropped to the floor. He transformed. He slowly lost his hair. Targ didn't have claws, long nails, fangs and a snout anymore! He was…a shade of pink in color! He was considerably smaller and appeared…helpless, pathetic.

"Oh, God," Blake said from the doorway and in a handsome suit.

The girl was *more than shocked* to see her young lover and his parents in ghastly, gruesome forms. She was terrified. She franticly shook. *This was totally unacceptable,* in her mind. *I'm marrying into THIS?!*

"Would you like to sit down, dear?" Soft, pink, pretty and human Emily asked in the same tone as the dinner conversation, as if nothing in the world was wrong.

Little Targ turned his human head toward his big, hairy lover and meekly said, *"Flem?"*

"AH!" Flem screamed as she slowly sat on one of the chairs.

"I'm sure you didn't expect this sort of thing,

tonight. Did you, Flem, dear?" Emily offered: "Tea? Cookies? Tacos?"

Flem shook her big head for NO and she shook for other reasons.

Targ assured her, "It will be all right, sweetie. Relax. Nothing to fear, darling. It's a normal thing around the Romanoff Castle, eh?"

Targ's betrothed grabbed a drink and gulped it down. She yelled, "Lord!" when the tea touched her large mouth. She threw the glass with full force. Flem gagged and growled questions: "Grrrrr! Why are you wearing, ah, what? Clothes?! Never mind. Grrrrr...*uh!* For how long will, will, will this last? And, and w-why?"

Blake informed her as if he again expressed a history lesson: "For the duration that the Moon is up and visible in the sky. We have hours before we return to normal. And only on the full Moon does this happen, dear. It will be tomorrow night as well..."

Flem cried and nervously asked: "This is, is g-going to happen tomorrow night, t-too?"

"You see, the oddest thing happened long ago. The real Lady Rothschild, the vampire and master of our liberator, must have had a 'kind spot' for one of the aliens. She 'kidnapped' a youngling human and materialized the alien baby here on Dragos..."

"What?" Flem asked but hardly listened. She was too dazed from her new reality for his words to register in her animalistic mind. She only saw red~.

Blake explained: "...But during the Great Purge, when all vampires were destroyed, the 'human' was found. The Lady must have loved the baby and kept the pink creature safely hidden away from her Lord and the other vampires that would surely have *killed it*. But that was only for a short time. On the day of the Purge, the baby was *eaten* upon discovery by a Wolf. That Wolf was my father. My father's sin and the *man-curse* have been passed down through every generation of our family, Flem. We hope you could understand?"

Targ sadly told her, "That goes for, for…our *children* as well, dear. They'll carry the curse also. But it's not so bad, dear. Really."

She suddenly and **violently tore apart every limb of the weak, puny, pink family in utter rage!** Then she mindlessly *ate most of the three Romanoffs!* She was full, but she fit them in. Later, she skulked through the moors of Dragos, still angered! Flem had no clue what she had done to herself out of blind hatred. She killed the last were-people on the planetoid. *"I'm never going to have a boyfriend! I'm never going to get married!"* Her violent act made her the only were-person on the planetoid. During the next full Moon in the night's sky, she will turn into a human being.

7 Jason and the Harpies

What IF there was a mutiny on the Argo and Jason was tossed overboard along with his stolen, useless, worthless, lifeless, Golden Fleece?

Hercules was behind the mutiny, thought Jason, now washed up on the far shores of Caulcas. *Of course, who else would be that brave and defy the gods? After Talos?* "Oh, Hera! What have I done?"

Jason was always a favored child by the gods. Very soon, the wind answered his question, but it was really Hera. She never left the boy's side. Her protection never wavered, yet the brave lad might not have thought so at the moment. What about his destiny, his future? He surely felt doomed at this time, abandoned by the gods?

Covered in wet sand on the shore, he coughed sea water out of his mouth. He took deep gulps of air to gain normal rhythm of breaths. He wiped his face, cleared his eyes and looked around. Then…

The wind whispered, *"Jason. What makes you think you have done wrong? The Fleece is not meant to hang in Troy, that's why its light and power died and sparked a mutiny on the Argo. Explore this side of the island. You will have the answers you seek. Keep the dark, ragged Fleece with you at all times. Remember: We on Olympus still watch the game and play it. It is far from over. Choose your thoughts and words carefully, my love. All is not lost. Good-bye."*

One more time, he went over recent events in his mind:

We were on our way back to Troy with the Golden Fleece. We got passed the Sirens; we escaped Harzaach, got passed his magic spells. All was good, a tremendously successful raid. We had the Fleece! We even released Siliphis from his cage, his torture by those flying, little harpy-devils. I'll never forget what he said: "I did not sin every day; why must I be tortured every day?"

Then, all the Argonauts turned against me and my driven-by-the-gods Quest! I was wrapped, tied to the Fleece and thrown overboard. I cursed every god in Mount Olympus!

"There it is." Jason said as he kicked sand on the thing with a ram's head. The lad worked himself free from it during the long swim. The Fleece floated and, "I can almost say the damn ram hair saved my life!"

The boy had been through a lot recently. It was a while since the feast at Harzaach's table. He could use a good meal. Jason felt exhausted from the swim. Hera said *explore this side of Caulcas.* "That, I will do." He rose to his feet and walked along the shores of the sea. He changed direction and went inland. An hour later, he was far from sea. Jason was within a grove of trees with a large clearing that looked familiar. Then, he heard a sound: a flutter of wings…

Completely without warning, a coconut dropped out of the sky and hit him perfectly on the top of his head! Jason was knocked out^.

When Jason came to consciousness and looked around, he saw that *he was caged!* In fact, he was in the same cage that Siliphis was locked inside and barely given a crumb of bread by the harpies. "Where *is* the guy? He owes me a big favor. And, where are those?"

"Ha, ha, ha, ha! What do we have here?" One of the small, dark-violet harpies said, right outside of the cage.

Then another one appeared. *"It looks like Jason of the Argo. How'd 'e get in 'ere? Ha, ha, ha!!"*

A third pesky critter flew in: *"Ah, how the mighty have fallen, ha, ha, haaaaa!"*

"Yes, you guys are very funny. Now, why don't you let me out?"

"We can see that you're hungry. We have something for you…"

"What is it?"

The harpy replied, *"It's a taco."*

"What's that?"

"You'll like it. Eat it! Ha, ha." It was tossed into the cage.

Jason picked it up. When he smelled it, he immediately dropped it. "Ugh. The skin might be edible, but not what's inside, thanks…"

"Ha, ha, ha, ha!"

"Oh, my. We're so funny! Why don't you tell him the good news?"

"Is it going to be bad news?" Jason asked.

"Yeah! Ha, Ha, ha!"

"Ha, ha…aaaaah."

"Here it is. King Harzaach is on his way here, right now!"

"Is that the truth?"

"It IS."

"We wouldn't lie 'bout that, Jason. He's coming to kill you! Really, for the Fleece."

"Really?"

"He doesn't know."

"Harzaach's skeletons killed the rest of the Argonauts. Your friends are all dead, Jason."

"They're dead, all of them?! But they headed back to Troy?"

"Hercules wanted blood and more and turned back. Foolishly he thought the Argonauts outnumbered the Caulcans and would easily win against them because they had no guards…"

"No visible guards, you see? His army waited underground, sleeping. Waited until wakened by blood and dragon's teeth."

"…When the crew returned to fight and establish a colony on Caulcas for Troy, the Sirens were ordered by the Wizard to let them pass. That's when they faced the skeleton soldiers and were all slaughtered."

"Hercules didn't know how powerful a wizard Harzaach is. Hercules' muscles were nothing against Dark Magic, aye?"

"Do you know how lucky you are, Jason? To not be with them. Thank the gods, boy…"

"Ain't that the truth. You'd be dead now."

You know, little ones, I think you are very right on that point. I do thank one particular Olympian game-player. Ha. Now that we've had this lovely and very informative chat…how about letting me out?"

"Sure. After you answer three questions correctly. Here's the situation. You better get your ass out of this area, quickly. There's a boat you can use. No lie. But you better get out soon. You see, the Fleece, and we have it in our possession, is not worthless. Once back in Harzaach's hands, it will light up and be as powerful as it ever was. So…2 situations: IF you get out of the cage, hats off to you sir, you deserve to present it to him and be a big hero in his eyes. That's all he wants: the Fleece, powerful magic in it. Ah! But, if we harpies present the Fleece to Harzaach, then, we're the big heroes and his skeleton army will literally eat you and spit you out in tiny pieces!"

"Really. They will. You better get out of the cage, man."

"Gimme the 3 questions!" Jason yelled. (It was the key).

"Oooh, goodie. Number 1: How were harpies created? How did we harpies come to be? Answer!"

"I thought everyone knew. You're a combination of demons and fairies."

"Damn! That's right!"

"You gotta make the questions harder!"

"Okay. Question 2: Who created us? Who mixed demon and fairy together? Answer!"

"I can only guess it was the Wizard Harzaach…"

"Damn! And fuck me!!"

"I told you to make them harder. There's only one more!"

"Ha, ha, ha." It was Jason's turn to laugh.

"Alright, the third question is an easy either/or question. 50-50 chance of getting it right, but I don't think you're gonna get it right. Here we go. Harzaach, King, Wizard, Magic-Man, whatever you want to call him…is he, under the rough/gruff exterior, a Demon-Hell Beast of pain and torture with no redeeming qualities at all…OR, under it all, at his core, is he really a misunderstood, softie and sweetheart?"

"He's really a misunderstood, softie, sweetheart. I

took a shot."

"E fucking got it right!! Damn, damn, damn! He figured it was a trick question! Let'm out."

The cage door swung open and Jason jumped out, fast. He immediately wrapped himself in the dark, ragged (still wet) Fleece. "Mmmm. Yes, it will be great when I give the Fleece to his Majesty. It's you guys that better scram from the area."

"When e's right, e's right, aye? Want another taco?"

"No. That's Okay. Ha, ha."

Jason truly became a great hero in the eyes of King Harzaach. The brave lad was allowed to sail home to Troy on the boat that was near shore. He had many stories to tell of his adventures on the Argo.

8 Robin Hoodlum

What IF the evil Sheriff of Nottingham hatched an insidious plot to ruin the good name of Robin Hood and marry Maid Marion?

It all began when he overhead a conversation between Marion and her #1 handmaid. The sheriff went to, once more, propose marriage to the beautiful/blonde Marion, who had always spurned his affections. Her heart was in love with that 'scoundrel,' Robin Hood, who of course, was truly not a scoundrel. He was a brave robber of the rich and giver to the poor. A famous and beloved *criminal,* but not to the authorities, whose leader was the Sheriff. Robin and his "merry" men were outlaws with prices on their heads.

The Sheriff stood behind Marion's door and heard her say to the handmaid: She would self-exile herself from Nottingham for one month and take secret residence with the nuns of Callay. No one would know where she was for a month. Her motives were to make Robin jealous and worried and, hopefully, have him marry her when she came out of hiding. The handmaid promised to keep her secret. The man turned right around and conceived of a "brilliant" plan.

Later, the Sheriff ordered that Friar Tuck be brought to him. He said to Tuck: "You personally feed prisoners in the dungeon, is that right, friar? I call it a dungeon."

"Indeed, I do, sir. I make sure the meals are, are…ah, *edible,* ah," the short, chubby man with no hair on top said.

The Sheriff insisted, "Well, there is one prisoner you will not attend to and feed in my jail cells. Guards are posted. You are to stay away from the cell with the guards. Is that clear, friar?"

"I shouldn't ask you: who it is, now, should I, sir?"

"No. No, you shouldn't. That is all. Now, go!"

When Friar Tuck dispensed the meals to sorry souls in the many individual cells called a "dungeon," he saw the guards. Two heavily-armed guards stood in front of a cell that was about 30 feet away from the other prisoners. Tuck went through the motions and fed people, while one eye was trained on the special prisoner. From what he made out, the prisoner was a woman with long blonde hair in a white gown. *Fascinating, hard to believe.* These gallows were meant for the most wretched lowlife criminals, not for a well-dressed woman who appeared as royalty.

Days later, one of the Sheriff's men was sent to find Robin Hood. It was in this portion of the forest that his band of outlaws was supposed to be and often fleeced the carriages of rich land barons. He walked farther and farther, all the while the guard was scared and knew he was watched. Up ahead was a small stream and a large log spanned its width and formed a bridge. When the guard reached the log, almost stepped on it, he saw three men dressed in green on the other side. They walked out from between trees. One was very large and carried a very big smile (Little John). He took the middle position and the other two flanked his sides. They all smiled. But not the Sheriff's guard.

"I don't want any trouble!"

Will Scarlett was on the right side of John. He asked, "Why are you here? Alone?"

"I carry a message for Robin Hood!" The guard placed a tied piece of parchment on the log and *ran back where he came from!*

Scarlett quickly loaded his bow with an arrow and SHOT.

Little John asked, "You're gonna nail 'im?"

He loaded another arrow from quiver and SHOT again. "Look at him run! No, I'm gonna miss him."

The other *merry* man grabbed the scroll from the far end of the log and gave it to Will, Robin's second in command.

When Scarlett read it, he exhaled in sadness. "Oh, no."

Later, Will spoke to Robin. Their leader with a red feather in his cap was incredibly distraught when he heard the news: *Maid Marion has been condemned to death by the throne of England for conspiring with Robin Hood and his men! Conditionally.*

"Robin! All of us have to do what the Sheriff has asked or *Marion's dead!* He's mad; he'll do it! If he can't have her, no one will! If you want to keep her alive, Robin, we all have to do our part."

"Will, it's insane! Robin Hood and his cheerful band of outlaws will now *rob from the poor?!* Any meager highwayman along the road and not royal carriages? Unthinkable! Everyone will hate me."

"I'm sure it's only temporary. Maybe Tuck can conceive of a plan, eh? The men are on your side; they'll go along with it. We can explain to our, our *victims*, aye…they'll get it back. It's all for the safety of Marion. Robin. Everyone loves Marion and knows of your love for her – you doing this for her. The people will understand and comply. Think about it."

"Aye. When you put it that way." Robin reluctantly agreed. "But, *fuck me*, we have to turn our booty in to the royals, aye? That's hard to live with, mate. There goes my legend. Now a legacy as a real criminal-crook by those who hear the tales later and don't know me for my real, honest intentions. I'm a fucking socialist! The Throne has abundance and *prints money!* Church and State should be *giving* us money! We're the poor! We're the ones who need it! Yes?"

"Preaching to the choir, mate. It'll be for a short time, Robin."

It was true and shocked a lot of fairly-poor highwaymen and their riders. Townsfolk were surprised to find Robin's men in green shout: "Stand and deliver!" to them. Some of the robbed victims were well acquainted with the Merry Men. A few were family with the beloved outlaws. But the news spread. They all believed Marion would be executed if Robin's men did not rob them. Most were happy to contribute to the cause and pitched in extra coins.

Robberies continued on the edge of Sherwood Forest. There were people who walked and rode the road of the forest, just to toss in pennies as a 'show,' to support Marion, Robin, and their love for one another. Robin was a hero to the people, and nothing will change that.

Robin, Will, John and others of the gang, said to average folk in carriages: "We don't really want to do this." Also: "We're very sorry, people; we would never usually do this to, to, to people like you." And: "We sure appreciate your donations, thank you very much. Maybe they'll be a slush-fund later and you'll get this all back, aye?"

It was late one evening. The night's sky was pitch black and there was much sadness among the men of Sherwood Forest. The gang was not merry. They've heard nothing from Friar Tuck who they assumed might have an insider's plan on getting Marion out of the 'dungeon.' But there was no word.

Just when the band's collective spirit was at its lowest (they couldn't even drink Mead), a miracle happened...

Sad faces, illuminated by the campfire, changed to happy faces, when Friar Tuck marched front and center, hand in hand, with Maid Marion!

"Wot's this?"

"She's free!"

"Tuck got her released!"

"No, bet 'e rescued 'er 'iself, 'e did!"

She ran to Robin's arms. They embraced and kissed.

He said, "Love you! I'm so happy, my love! Friar

got you out…"

"No, no, Mister Locksley. I was away on holiday, only the Sheriff knew. He fooled everyone with my handmaid in prison in one of my wigs. He knew the friar would see her from a distance and think it was me. With all the rumors the Sheriff spread, everyone thought I was in desperate peril and made you do what you did. I love you, too."

"Wot?"

"Blimey."

The wonderful reunion between lovers was topped off one late evening when the Sheriff was *kidnapped* and brought to Sherwood Forest to be "best man" at the wedding between Robin and Marion! He was forced to witness their marriage, performed by Friar Tuck. She wore green and a cap with a red feather. Her and the friar were now outlaws and would live in the forest. Marion could have been royalty with more riches and more servants. She traded it all for love.

9 IF Bruce Wayne was Superman & Clark Kent was Batman

Yes, what would happen IF a surreal universe existed where Clark Kent came from a Bat World planet, and "flew" to Earth at a young age. He became extremely strong because of the different sun. He became the Caped Crusader and wore black and gray. And Bruce Wayne was a brilliant, rich, super-detective, and maybe the smartest man on Earth. With incredible gadgets and a red and blue costume, he assumed the persona of "Superman," because he was a super-man.

In Metropolis, Inspector Henderson called the residence of Bruce Wayne. The billionaire inventor was informed that a "riddle" was left on his door from the Riddler and it read: *What's the first thing the Bat thinks of when he thinks of me?* "Can you translate it, sir?"

Bruce replied, "I think I can, inspector. I think of the

Riddler as a joker. It might mean the Riddler and Joker are now working together on some villainy? Please keep me informed if there are any more."

"I will, Superman."

In Gotham City…

"Chief. I think it's time for the bat-signal. The Riddler and the Joker have teamed up, it seems. Don't you think we should call the Caped Crusader, sir?"

"I agree," Gotham's chief of police said to the sergeant.

Signal was sent and a huge Bat-Image was projected in the sky.

Batman was already at work for the public and flew up and retrieved a cat who was stuck in a tree when he saw the bat-signal. As soon as he placed the cat in its owner's hands, he flew off at lightning speed toward city hall…

In the 6th floor window of the Chief of Police zipped Batman, furiously, like he always did. He knew how to make an entrance.

"Bugs me when you do that, Batman! Scares the willies in me."

"What do you mean?"

The frustrated Chief asked: "Can't you run here real fast and not do that? I'm sure you could?"

Batman smiled and said, "I'm a bat. Bats fly, no?"

Suddenly, Superman opened the door and walked into the room.

"What the hell's he doing here?"

"Let me explain, I know you two don't get along. Since Riddler and Joker have teamed up, I thought you two could join forces and solve the case? Something's going down. We got another riddle."

The two superheroes stared at one another.

Bruce (Superman) asked, "What's the new riddle?"

The Chief replied, "What has a mouth and sounds like 'crook.'"

"Let's see," Clark (Batman) said and scratched his cowl (side of his head).

Superman (Bruce) replied, "The answer is brook, as in water, a stream, river. Further, I can conclude something is going down at the Brooke Oil Refinery, which is located at the mouth of Gotham River. Also, it's owned by the Joker. One of his legitimate businesses."

Clark, all muscles, said with a scowl: "You think you're so damn smart, don't ya? Super-*man.*"

Chief said, "Now, now, Batman. I think Superman nailed it. The refinery should be investigated, soon as possible."

Batman was cocky and casually said, "Then, I'll just fly there and surprise the living daylights out of the bad guys, Aye?"

"NO. That's exactly what we should not do! The riddle was too easy; it's a trap. We don't rush in! We sneak in slowly and stake out the joint, first," Bruce said, confidently.

"What?" "What?"

"Look, Chief. This team of yours will work if he realizes who's the brains and who's the brawn? I almost like the guy; gotta million questions for him, for anyone who thinks he's a bat-*man...*"

"Hey! Supe! You know I could huff and puff and blow that head of yours off? Where would you be without your head!?"

"Boys. Boys! Don't fight, please. I'll bet one day you'll be friends. C'mon, now. Let's solve one together, eh?"

"Okay."

"I'm willing to be nice, if he will?" The boys exchanged smiles.

"There you go." The Chief was happy and clapped his hands.

Bruce, the Man of Steel (Will), said, "Tell you what, Bat. Ride with me, we have time. Can have a little chat; get to know one another better? What do you say, Caped Crusader?"

"Ah." Batman looked at the Chief and thought he should agree. "You mean…in the Supermobile?" Batman's eyes lit up a bit…

And so did Superman's. "Yeah, yeah. Bet you want to ride in the Supermobile? I'll even let you drive…"

"You will!?" Then Batman was less excited. "Sure. That be fine."

"You can drive a cool car. Gotta lot of features and badass toys attached to it. Just don't go too fast. Hair-trigger. Whatever the fuck you drive."

"What?"

"Said, feels like yer really alive! Supermobile. Thought bats had super-hearing?"

Clark in black and gray and Bruce in red and blue, sped along the freeway by the river. Batman drove. It was a very dark night.

"Tell me about your planet, alien-man. A Bat World?"

"Look, lucky bitch, your Earth is bright and filled with millions of types of animals. Beautiful, colorful animals. We have only bats! We have rocks and a lot of darkness. We use their shit; it's a *big resource.* Anyway, we discovered that our kind <u>thrived in space</u>, we lived on microwaves and cosmic rays! We only had the ability to send one person and a small ship into space. That was me at a young age. But the computer told me your yellow Sun would give me superpowers. Back on Dragos, our sun was purple and we hardly saw it. Sure enough, when I got here…I was a Super Bat! Only I *needed* to be super 'cos I crashed the ship near the north pole."

"That's a heck of a story, Batman. I still don't get the bat theme, but I can sure understand now, since they were so important to your culture, *keep your eyes on the road!*"

"Oh!" The Supermobile swerved.

"You're not blind as a bat, now?"

"No, I have super-eyesight," Batman said.

Superman said, "Good. My story is I come from old money. You see the estate I live on. I was spoiled; had the best training, teachers. It was easy for me to be *years* ahead of anyone in my class. Hell, I was ahead of everyone in my special class! I went to work and invented toys I loved and, as it turned out, they made me into a *superhero*. No car is like the one you're driving, buddy. I have jetpacks in the suit. I fly too, for short periods. It's new, not perfected. I was thinking of a partner, some youth I could train, an apprentice. A few very athletic boys at the Youth Center. Ha, I'd call him the Boy Wonder. Ha, ha."

Batman said, "That's so stupid. *Boy Wonder?* Ha! Are you gay?"

"Yeah, well. I mean, no, I'm not. Hey, what kid wouldn't envy ridin' shotgun with me when my Super Computer sends us out on…?"

"You don't hide who you are, Bruce, like I do.

Everyone knows who you are. Ego-maniac," Clark said.

Bruce replied, "Man, you're so stupid. You really think you are fooling anyone with the muscles, mask and deep voice, Bat? Everyone at the Planet knows you're Batman. You think Lois hasn't sussed you out, mate? Ha. Seriously? Man, you're batty."

Clark was pissed. He said, "Sign says Brooke Oil."

"We're here."

Later, Superman pointed to where he'd jet up to the refinery roof.

"I'll save you the trouble." Batman grabbed him and flew him up to the top and over. They landed on a perch that overlooked the main factory that had the most lights around it. In broad darkness it was the Joker. Batman saw him as plain as day. Superman couldn't, because he didn't have super-sight.

"What's he doing?" Superman asked.

"Oh, my God. He has a bomb!" Batman yelled. "I'm going…"

"No, you're not!" Superman jumped on Batman. Clark could have easily broken free, but he listened to Bruce. "Chief said, I'm in charge. This is not right. It's a trap, just like I figured…"

"How do you figure that? If all the oil goes up?!"

"Listen!" Superman insisted. "Joker was always gunning for you. You're the one he's after, not me. Why destroy his own refinery? It's not even insured. We arrived just at this critical time? Why didn't he do it an hour ago or ten minutes ago? Do you ever use your brain, Batman, or are you all muscle? I think I'll go down and talk to him."

"You're the batty one, Bruce, if you think I'll let you beat me to the punch." With that, he flicked Bruce in the face with a finger...

"Hey! Ow."

There was no stopping the Caped Crusader. He flew down, under refinery lights, and confronted the Joker.

On the ledge, Superman yelled, "Nooooo!" Then said, "I better get down there." He climbed down; the jetpack was on the fritz. Bruce heard insane laughter in the black background and recognized it. It was the high-pitched laugh of the Riddler.

Batman, coolly/casually, walked toward the Joker. He noticed his archenemy only now lit the (dud) bomb's fuse. "This is too easy." 💣

Suddenly, Joker, from his back pocket, pulled out a fresh/potent branch of WOLFSBANE! Wolfsbane, the bane of the bat! His one weakness. The one thing that rendered him powerless and could eventually kill the Dark Knight! *He fell down to the ground, drained of energy.* One more minute, and it will be fatal.

Joker screamed in joy, utter rapture! "I finally found out about wolfsbane and I got my hands on gobs of it in its purest form. Here, Bat. I've prepared a whole wolfsbane pie for you; you'll love it!" The Joker grabbed the pie and also heard distant laughs from his new partner. He was ready to smash Batman's face with the pie, when...

Flying gizmos Superman invented struck the Joker like bullets. They had fishlines on them and wrapped around his body, tightly. He was caught. The Riddler ran away. Superman pulled a super-vacuum from his utility belt, sucked up the wolfbane and incinerated it. He said, "Clark, do I always have to fly in and save you? Ha, ha, ha."

Clark laughed along with his new super friend.

10 What Happened to Braniac 5?

IF only Brainiac 5 did not shrink the "Bottled City of Kandor."

But he did, and certainly paid the consequences for his actions. Few people know his story. Green-skinned Brainiac 5, 5th in a series of humanoids run by computer mainframes, was an archenemy to Jor-El, Ka-El's (Superman's) father on Krypton. They stood in opposition because Jor-El voted against *political decisions made-by-machines,* and Brainiac 5 led the charge for a Machine takeover and nearly all systems run by machines, which eliminated the human-factor.

The 'Machine Amendment' was universally voted-down by the people of Krypton and Five was arrested and thrown in prison for "treasonous acts" and other criminal acts. He was confined for a very long time. He vowed to have his revenge on Jor-El and his family.

Five's lifespan was extremely long and he outlived his sentence. When he was eventually released, the evil madman went to work on his plan:

Brainiac 5 knew that Jor-El's hometown was Kandor and Kandor was one of the most beautiful cities on Krypton. He could have wiped out the entire city with an old Death Ray device that he got to function. But no. Brainiac 5 wanted to be far cleverer than simply destruction. He wanted to be BRILLIANT and have Jor-El suffer by seeing the Kandorian's agony day after day. So, the emerald super-genius invented a massive Shrink Ray. From a high canyon wall, under a very red sun, he aimed the Ray-Gun at Kandor, down in the valley below. The whole city **shrunk in size** in a short time. Jor-El sent his best scientists there and they were able to preserve and protect the city from further harm. It was encased within a clear structure that resembled a 'bottle.'

Brainiac's terrible crime of revenge was not good enough for the madman. He went forward in time, discovered what children Jor-El had spawned and then he waged a few battles with Kal-El on Earth, after he found out Jor-El's son was a superhero and super-powered on a planet with a yellow sun. For a strange reason, which might have to do with 5's mechanical core and not a bio core, *Brainiac was not super* when he arrived on Earth. He used his machines to fight Superman and he lost. His great wits were no match against Kal-El's great strength. Kal-El's brain was also made super because of the Earth-Sun. In the end, Superman won!

In the battle against Brainiac, Superman was able to use 5's time-vortex, a tunnel he used to get from Krypton to Earth. When Kal-El arrived on the solid, intact, planet of his father, he was not super. But he had the ability to carry the shrunken city with him when he returned to Earth. When he returned to Earth, his super powers also returned, and in his hands, he held a precious piece of home world that he thought was lost forever.

Superman preserved and protected Kandor, just like his father did long ago. He kept it safe in his Fortress of Solitude near the north pole. It was not a "constant reminder of suffering." The little supermen and superwomen were permanently sealed inside the "bottle" and could not leave the confinement. It was just as well. They lived and died normal lives, while always under the watchful eyes of Superman. Even super men and women eventually die.

What to do about Brainiac 5? There was no prison on Earth or one that Superman could construct better than the Phantom Zone. Kal-El didn't want to ever see his father's enemy again after what he experienced in his fight with 5. He pushed the black button on the old, red machine and the machine sent Brainiac to the Phantom Zone><.

TS Caladan

11 The 7 Faces of Dr. No

IF Doctor No, after being defeated and disgraced by James Bond, went in a whole new direction with his life…

Today, the Doctor was very old and had two things on his mind after his rocket deal went up in smoke because of 007:

He wanted to turn Jewish because he always felt that he was a good Jew, deep inside. Also, he wanted to own a circus. It was a childhood fantasy of his ever since gypsies passed through his first home, a village in Outer Maldavia. No longer imprisoned, and plenty rich from wise investments, he was free and pursued his dreams.

One point that must be made: Doctor No, after his confinement in a federal prison for 10 years, became gay. He was very gay and proud of his new lifestyle. Now, he had flair. He dressed in colorful, casual, soft-to-the-touch robes.

He set up auditions for special kinds of acts in New York City. After careful examination of the performers he wanted for his circus, he chose…

A CHPs officer on his motorcycle to be the lead singer and MC. He chose a COWBOY, CONSTRUCTION WORKER, an INDIAN, a BIKER, a MILITARY MAN and finally, a MUSCLE MAN. Doctor No was uncertain if the acts would be appreciated in Outer Maldavia.

12 Plans 1 – 8 from Outer Space

IF only the alien Aldebarans used their first ideas for ruling Earth rather than their 9th Plan of raising the dead, they may have been more successful? But remember, these particular Aldebarans weren't smart.

Plan 1: Communicate with gorillas and convince them to be the alien's army. When proposed, a silverback threw his shit at the aliens.

Plan 2: Through media, create a fictional "virus," a new Black Plague to cause world chaos! But they realized: Who'd believe it?

Plan 3: Turn everyone gay by a constant broadcast of 'Cats.'

Plan 4: Destroy all sources that made the production

of tea possible. Then they realized many Earthlings might thank them.

Plan 5: Zap all marijuana fields and destroy its THC, rendering the "new medicine" useless. Due to drastic miscalculations, the aliens actually increased pot's potency by a factor of 10.

Plan 6: Kill all cute, little cats to break the hearts of owners. But when the cats found out, they put their paws down and didn't allow it.

Plan 7: Place a spell on humans that made them *believe* the crap that was broadcast from television sets. Then, the Aldebarans realized that the Earthlings already believed the crap from television sets.

Plan 8: The aliens planned to end all beautiful memories of days gone by, the friendliness of neighbors when they cared and gave and were wonderful people, the kindness that was in most people's hearts. Then, they found out that the good memories were already forgotten.

13 Forbidden Moon

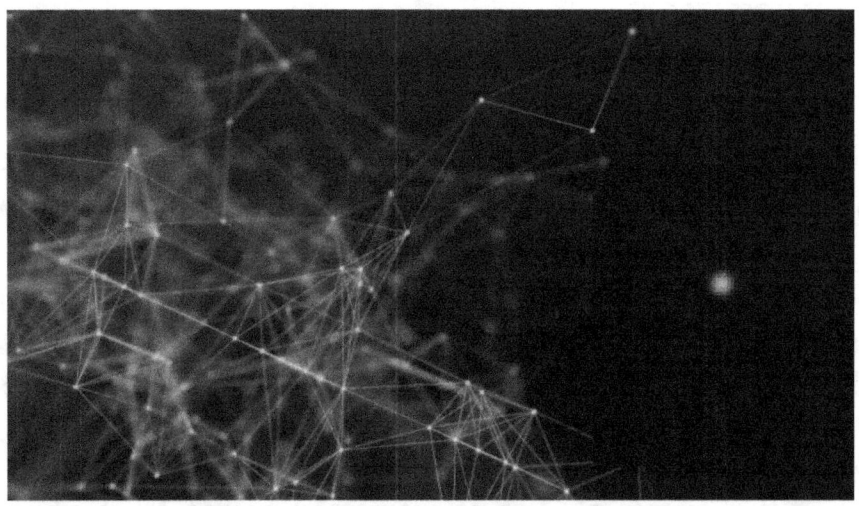

What IF the Martian satellite, Deimos, is not what you think it is?

"Sir. I've only recently reached level 10 clearance. The soldiers with a 10-level clearance are aware of the incident on Deimos…"

"And, you'd like to be let in on what happened to the Blerafon?"

"Yes, Magistrate."

"I don't see why not, Officer Joorma. It is the talk of the base. The Blerafon, as all of Mars knows, was sent to explore what we call 'Deimos,' because of its sudden appearance. Mars has no moons, but now we do. This fact has spread through Media channels, even though Deimos is too small to be seen by any of our eyes. I want you to see it in the multi-scope, then I'll go on with what happened…"

"Sure."

The Magistrate and officer walked on their 5 legs over to the multi-scope, a multi-scope fitted for many-eyed creatures.

"Take a look, Joorma. Tell me what you see?"

"Ah, Okay. It'll take a moment to fit them all in…"

"You'll fit them in."

"Alright. I see. *What is that?!* I assume that's Deimos to the right. What's that thing? On the left? My goodness…it's moving?"

"It's *growing.* The general Flarg population doesn't know about the Talosion Shield that is extending and extending a little more each day between us and this bizarre rogue moon of mystery."

"It's purpose, sir?"

"It prevents any of us interested Flargs from going there, or will when it's fully formed."

Jooma asked, "Is Deimos really irregular-shaped, Magistrate?"

"Yes. It is rough, made of titanium, iron ore and zinc, primarily."

"About the Blerafon, sir?"

"Right. No communications between the visitors, if lifeforms were on the sudden moon, and our leaders. *Nothing.* So, we had volunteers willing to travel there to see what's up and report back, if they could? The ship landed and discovered an amorphous creature that constantly changed. If you think some of us insectoids appear hideous, you should see what Morphias looked like, eh?"

"Morphias?"

"That's what the big/colorful blob called himself. Everything was going great until one of the troops walked into his daughter-blob…"

"What?"

"The aliens are soft like jelly. When he accidently walked through to her middle, she started to *SPRITZ like a gin fizz!* Morphias took it as a sexual violation and sent his ID out after the Blerafon crew."

"What's an ID?" the officer asked the Magistrate.

"Okay, this is what's hard to believe, only for those who know Top Secrets…"

"What?"

"The entire Deimos satellite, which appears like another rock in space, is *actually alive.* Truth is the massive creature looks nothing like what we see. It could fly away from orbit at millions of miles a second, but it chooses not to, for some reason. Everyone was killed there on the moon's surface by the Blob. You see why the Shield?"

"I'm sorry to hear the news, sir. Yes, I see. There are a few Flarg corporations with private space programs. It's certain they know of Deimos and have designed missions to visit it. Probably."

"They can't now. I stand corrected. All was not wiped out by Morphias. He liked Robbie, the ship's android navigator and computer. He stole that and allowed Robbie to send a message back. That's how we know what happened…along with a *warning* to never attempt another landing."

"Are we sending another mission, Magistrate?"

"Hell, yes, we're sending another ship to Deimos! Dammit!"

The Blerafon II landed on Deimos, quietly, without incident. Captain Nielson ordered his men to spread out in all directions and use the radio if there was anything to report. The men followed orders.

Then Robbie appeared over a sand dune. It was a very fast, wheeled version of the android, with a trailer. He picked up the intelligent, 5-footed "Martians" and brought them all to where Morphias was located.

"Gentlemen! *No women, huh?* I welcome you!" the colorful blob, who spoke for the Living Satellite, shouted.

"Aren't you going to project your mind and kill us too, Morphias?" Captain Nielson asked. He didn't know where to look; it didn't have a face.

"Oh, that was a long time ago. I'm different now. I have learned a lot since then. I'm also a proud grandfather! When one of you critters contacted my daughter, *she got preggers!* Okay. Bring him out here!"

The Flargs looked around. Suddenly, a thing materialized before them that was half-blob and half-Flarg. *It was the most disgusting thing these Martians had ever seen.*

"I see this doesn't please you. Send him away." It disappeared.

Captain Nielson asked, "We want to know why you are here, in orbit. We can forgive the disastrous incident of First Encounter, that can be chalked up to a big misunderstanding. What do you want? The Flargs of my planet want to know what you are doing here?"

"Oh, I can answer that. We're *hiding*. I have an enemy. An archenemy. We happen to appear much the same, the bastard. It's like a game of Hide and Seek, only it's for our *lives*. We're playing a…"

"**CAUGHT YOU!**" That means, I've won this round!" Phobos screamed with utter joy. "But I am magnanimous, brother! I won't shatter you to tiny pieces! I *will* render you inert, cold, lifeless, devoid of all energy/power, trapped in this orbit." Phobos continued: "And I will also orbit Mars right along with you, brother! My obelisk will keep you in check, in position, so I can always look upon my brother Deimos, and know that I have won. What's it feel like to lose, loser?!"

14 The Day Mars Stood Still

IF Mars was at an extremely critical point in its human history and the Martians were visited and warned by a Space Ranger and his very powerful robot.

One day on Mars, a day with bright blue skies and green grass and turquoise oceans…

A sound was heard over the Martian capital of Cydonia. It was a *buzzing* sound that none of the humans ever heard before. The sound got louder and louder and soon an object was seen in the clear air over Central City.

It passed over the prime power pyramid and the Giant Face that looked upward and appeared to welcome those from space.

The round object passed over thousands of people, and traveled lower and lower until it landed on the doorstep of City Hall. A huge crowd watched its slow descent and soon surrounded the spacecraft. It was a silver saucer that shined in the yellow sunlight. Was the unannounced, unexpected visitor a hostile invader? *Are we at war?*

Immediately. Robot-defense systems went into action and a multitude of guns and weapons were trained on the unknown probe.

Then, suddenly, a door in the craft opened...

A 10-foot tall, silver android walked out of the opening and took a few mechanical steps out onto the spaceship. In two seconds, red laser lines and a few blue ones struck different parts of a *thing* that had very few physical features. It was awkward, clunky and moved very slowly. The lasers (on force 100) had no effect at all and did not stop the robot's movements. The android came to an abrupt stop and remained motionless. More lasers hit it and then the weapon-fire stopped. Hundreds of people backed away from the craft. Thousands observed the scene from crystal towers in the Martian metropolis.

After moments of panic and fear, a tall man in a spacesuit and helmet walked out of the opening in the ship! This was the pilot and he had a device that will broadcast his words to the crowd and also a device that increased his psi-abilities so telepaths in the audience heard his message and understood.

"My name is Lattu and I am a Ranger, a

representative from police forces you are not aware of. We patrol the galaxy, monitor problems that could threaten neighboring systems and extinguish them. You all know of the Civil War that is presently raging by red rebels against the old blue regime. We Rangers see the future and know of coming events. We see how what you do today affects the future and changes it. Because of the red coup that has taken control now, rebels intend to destroy the 5th planet as a show of force, as a sign of their great power. We cannot allow that. The natives of Lilith are lovely, beautiful, innocent creatures and we will not permit their destruction. I have come with an ultimatum for the red side of the war. Stop this insane war, make peace with the blue regime and end all hostilities, and your planet and all you know will not be destroyed. *Or,* continue your rebellion, continue building your 'big gun' planet-killer that threatens every world in your system, and our response will be automatic. You see before you a G.A.I., which is our Global Automatic Instrument. If you continue your warlike ways, the G.A.I. will have no choice and will ravage Mars until it is a totally burned-out cinder in space. The choice is yours. …Also, we've brought you a gift. With this…"

Red lasers struct the small device in Lattu's hand and it *exploded*. A few more red lasers hit his body and helmet and had no effect.

"I was saying, with this, a device where you could speak to other inhabitants in your solar system, this, ah…it could have been used for peace. But now, now you've destroyed it. *Ugh.* We wait to hear from the rebels. Will they cease and desist their plans for conquest?" Lattu was disgusted by what happened so far that he went back into the ship through the opening. The opening closed.

The G.A.I. moved. It scared the vast crowd and the entire planet since everyone watched Martian media at the moment. The tall android slowly, carefully walked off the spaceship and reached the ground. It stood there, motionless, and stayed motionless. In minutes, the crowd was slightly less fearful.

Later, Lattu sat at his computer console where he communicated with other Rangers instantly and compensated for the time dilation.

"I don't know what's wrong with Martian society, sirs. How could they have let paradise fall to ruin? How could rebels even come to exist in what was once a fantastic utopia…?"

"Such rich and wonderful human history the colony has experienced over millennia. For this rebel-punk manifestation to appear and grow, a movement for violence and bloodshed, instead of peace and good will…it's unthinkable. How fast they have fallen…"

"I have not lost hope, sirs…"

"What do you plan, Officer Lattu?"

"I plan to go out among Martians, see how the average person lives. Maybe gain some insight on recent events? Who knows? I have to do something during what could be a long wait."

"Best of luck, officer. I know you will report when you have something to report. Base out."

"Out."

Later in the day, the human from another world removed his protective suit and "beamed" into a lane between buildings. He wore average Martian clothes and was a handsome man. No one could tell he was a man from another world.

He came upon a residence with a Blue Dot, much like other domed residences, except those marked with a Red Dot. [Politics] A sign on the wall advertised "room for rent." He entered…

Lattu found a family at their dinner table and his appearance frightened them. "I'm sorry if I startled you, I saw the room for rent."

"Come in, come in…Mister?" the old man asked, nervously.

He had to improvise fast and said, "My name is Wood. Armiston Wood and it's a pleasure to meet you."

The old man introduced: "I'm Tap and this is my wife Edg and my son, Jak. My oldest child is upstairs and getting ready for a date. I'm sure the room we have will suit you. Well, I hope it will, sir."

Jak was a young boy and expressed exuberance. "Are you here 'cos of the spaceman?! I'll bet he is, dad!"

Edg said: "Don't bother the nice man, Jak."

Tap said: "Now, now, son. You're so excited, but, ha, ha, most of us are just plain scared about the invasion."

The man's daughter walked down the steps, and…

"Oh, this is Coffee, my oldest one. We have a renter for the room; his name is Mister Wood."

She was a very pretty lady and was instantly attracted to Mr. Wood. Coffee walked to him, extended her arm and they shook hands. There was chemistry in the touch. It was as if she'd known him from some other life. "Glad to meet you, Mister Wood." Big smiles.

Lattu also felt a connection with the woman, as if he was fated to meet her. He said, "Call me: Armi. I'm a businessman and new in town. Only here for a short stay. Lovely home."

"Thank you," she replied with bright eyes.

"Sis, you promised to take me to town today. You promised."

Tap and Edg rolled their eyes. They knew her sudden date was more important than the boy's day out. Her date was with a politician.

Mr. Wood suggested: "Maybe you'd allow *me* to take the boy to town? He could show me around. I'd like to see the sites before I leave. If that's alright, of course?"

They had good feelings toward the stranger and it was agreed.

"Good. It's settled, then."

Jak was happy and said, "Yay."

Jak and Mr. Wood viewed the amazing white domes, gold buildings and crystal towers around them. Lattu saw how structures had red dots and some contained blue dots. Red far outnumbered the blue. He asked: "Jak? The rebel movement? Can you tell me how or why people are falling for it? Rebels mean to take over and kill. Why are you, why are they not protesting against the New Wave, even fighting them? I would imagine there are millions of good Martians who resist. Why do they have no power to stop them and have allowed the rebellion to grow?" The Space Ranger thought his question was too broad, too deep for the boy to give a coherent answer. He was wrong.

Jak said, "I think it's because of fear."

(Jak may have been very right and given the proper response).

Mr. Wood grabbed his jaw and rubbed it in thought.

He asked, "Jak? Who's the most intelligent person in the world, or in the area?"

"My father's pretty intelligent. Oh, you mean, like a scientist?"

"Yeah. Can you take me to your top scientist? Is that possible?"

"Suppose that would be, ah, Doctor Dinn. He's at the university and the university is right there, up a ways. Sure am having fun with you, Mr. Wood. You're a kook…"

"Ha, ha. Kooky, am I? Ha. Let's go see the doctor."

State officials from the red and blue sides convened at the G.A.I. robot that still stood motionless at the base of City Hall. They encased it within a force 100 forcefield. Both sides believed the thing was neutralized.

A half hour later, the boy took Lattu inside a massive, domed amphitheater. Mr. Wood looked up Doctor Dinn's room # in the lobby directory. Jak agreed to stay in the lobby and stay out of trouble.

The doctor's door was locked, but not for the spaceman. He opened it in seconds. He walked down an aisle between classroom seats and approached a large board at the front of the room.

"Ha, ha, ha! The God Particle, the key to quantum physics, he'll never find it that way." Lattu erased a set of figures and formulae on the left and wrote in different numbers and quotients.

"See here! What's the meaning of this?!" the doctor screamed.

"I simply wanted to help you reach the solution, doctor. Figures on the left do not matter, they cross each other out. This is what matters: Not MC squared, MC cubed, a 3-way crossfire. There. You should be able to see 'God' very soon now, Doctor Dinn." Smiled.

The old, white-haired doctor was very, very pleased. And greatly honored. "Let me guess. You are Lattu and dropped in on us, earlier in the day? You are the spaceman, yes?"

"I am indeed, sir."

"Ah. I have a few million questions to ask you. I'm curious."

"Ha, ha. Curiosity makes the best science, doctor."

"Wait! I have a marvelous thing to show you. It's just happened! Don't you know?"

"What is that, doctor?"

"Look." The old Martian opened his window and the view was of a distant scene of android troops, the vast RED Army, robot-machines that usually poured out of black factories and stood in such contrast to the beautiful domes, golden buildings and the crystalline towers. "They've stopped!"

"Stopped?" Lattu asked.

"Production. Maybe your message was received and heeded? Endless war-weapons flow from the black factories every day, but now, they've stopped. It must be a good sign. Don't you think it's a good sign, my friend?"

The visitor smiled. "Could be? I've received no word so far, no final confirmation. I'm still waiting, sir. I should go."

Doctor Dinn grabbed Lattu's hand and shook it with joy. "I am very happy to have met you, Lattu. Thank you for your help. Ah."

"Been a great pleasure for me as well, doctor. Good-bye."

"Good-bye."

When the spaceman and the boy returned to Jak's dome home, Lattu spoke to Coffee alone. She told him the breaking news, news that was also received over his devices. She said, "Rebels have given their answer and they believe the spaceman is bluffing. The radicals are proceeding with their plan for the Big Gun, I'm afraid…"

"No, that is very wrong. They cannot move forward with their plan. Coffee, it truly means the end of everything on your planet…"

"How can you be so sure, Mister Wood?"

"Because I am Lattu. I am your spaceman, Coffee. And the robot responds automatically. I have no control over it. It will kill you all!"

Coffee backed away from him. Her heart told her he truly was the spaceman. When she viewed his speech to the Martian population, she was moved. She knew Lattu only tried to do the right thing, to help. And now she felt it. The lady relaxed, calmed herself and held his hand. She felt love. "What can we do?" Coffee asked in desperation.

It was the end of the world on Mars. Yet, Lattu smiled and asked her: "How would your family like to take a ride with me?"

Maybe she sensed it was the end of the world. Her heart said: "Yes! We'll go with you."

The G.A.I. activated and crashed through the force 100 forcefield with ease. It slowly looked around. People in the area screamed and ran for their lives! The robot opened its visor, slowly, then looked around. Suddenly, a very **wide/purple Death Ray shot out** and melted golden buildings, white domes and crystal towers as if they were plastic!! In a short time, Central City was a wiped blob of goo. The G.A.I. marched and covered little ground, but *every beautiful construction from horizon to horizon was destroyed!!* It marched on…

The Space Ranger had no choice in the matter: He had to leave the G.A.I. to do its large-scale annihilation. But the man could choose to save a few Martians and took Edg, Tap, Coffee and Jak on as passengers aboard his silver saucer. Lattu took them to his Ranger base on his planet. Soon, he would be onto the next assignment.

Jak was thrilled!

Consequences of the robot's actions were *mixed*. On one hand, a few refugees escaped world destruction and migrated to the 3rd planet in the system and started the Atlantis colony. A family was saved and in for wild adventures. Most importantly: Wondrous beings on the 5th planet were spared from total genocide! Also, the Rangers knew the future – if the Martian Gun was initiated, calculations were wrong and the feedback-effect would have *decimated Mars,* made it red with radiation and unlivable. Fragments from the Event now never formed an Asteroid Belt around the Sun, never blasted away bits and damaged inner planets, or shot far out at tremendous velocities and created comets that returned, or created the Kuiper Belt of slow particles that never returned. Earth will never see fireballs and shooting stars><.

15 Zorro, Lost in Space

IF Guy Williams, who played Zorro on TV, was brought onboard the Jupiter II and exchanged places with Guy Williams, who played John Robinson in 'Lost in Space,' what might happen?

"What is this junk you and the robot have gathered and tossed here? You'll have to clean it up, you know?" Doctor Smith asked.

"This isn't junk, Doctor Smith," Will replied. "They are components of the ship that I've cannibalized; we don't need these conducers and condensers, see?"

"I don't see why you've piled them here?"

The robot said, *"Patience, doctor. All comes to us if we wait long enough."*

"He's a Chinese philosopher now, eh?" The doctor frowned.

"Ha, ha." Will laughed then explained: "I think I can make a special kind of teleporter, that is, if I can successfully drain enough of the ship's power."

"To do what, boy?"

"Well, Dr. Smith, how would you like a teleporter to beam you to Earth? But I'm not sure if it will work...?"

Robbie shook its mechanical arms and yelled a bit: *"It will work! It will work!"*

Doctor Smith changed his attitude. "That's *marvelous,* Will. Well, then, I will leave you at it. Gotta go. You tell me if you need my help." Smith waved, then walked out.

"Yes, Doctor Smith. I will." Inside, Will Robinson laughed. He said to the robot: "I'm still not sure about this. So many calculations. I have faith in the equipment. We need something to latch onto from Earth, some signal, then, *maybe* we can home in and get home?"

The next day, the machine was assembled and *activated,* but the energy siphoned from the spaceship only came in a small stream. The teleporter would take hours to generate enough power to send a person across lightyears of space. They waited.

John Robinson was very proud of his son and his "Hail Mary" attempt to get them back to Earth in a very unconventional way. He brought his wife, Maureen, and his daughter, Penny, into the lab section of the ship and showed-off Will's device. The mechanism was wide and tubular and stood on 3 legs. It hummed.

Maureen was amazed, but didn't believe it. *"This* is going to get us back home?? You sure, John? Ha, ha, that boy of ours..."

"Is it safe? That's what I want to know," Penny asked.

The father and husband chuckled. He said, "I trust

the robot. He would never let anything hurt us. We'll see what he says, aye?"

"Wouldn't it be something, to be broadcast back to Earth?" Maureen smiled, and day-dreamed, then blew a kiss to John.

John smiled back, winked and *accidentally touched the device!*

HE WAS SUCKED INTO THE MACHINE!!! As if he was only magnetic photons, he disappeared with a sudden "whoosh!"

His family was shocked and froze in silence for a moment.

Then…HE RETURNED!

But…the man was dressed completely different and he wore a MASK! A black mask around his eyes and a black cape! He had a thin mustache. It looked like John, only his skin was a shade darker and his black hair was greasy (shiny).

"My God, John. You disappeared! Then you reappeared a few seconds later, *like this?"*

Penny also had wide eyes and an opened mouth. She asked, "Dad? Were you at a costume party? What happened?"

"Who are you!?" The costumed man said in a slightly Spanish accent. "Dad? I'm not your father, little girl…"

"John?" Maureen was frightened.

"John?" he echoed back. "I am not…*John.* I am Don Diego! Well, well, not in this outfit. In this outfit, *I am Zorro!* The masked…" It was then that Don Diego, aka Zorro, took a good look around him. He had no conception of what his eyes viewed: Sleek, slick counters, white curved walls, odd/little lights that flashed, machines he didn't understand, strangers in strange clothes, and most of all: a tubular device on three legs. "Where am I?"

It was then that Will walked into the lab along with Robbie.

"Dad? Oh, no. Did my machine do this?" Will was frightened.

"Will? You did this? How…what?" his mother asked. She shook.

The robot explained: *"Transporter was set to an old transmission from Earth as to form a solid conduit of transport. I viewed a Spanish town on the other end and set the machine properly, only waiting power build-up to…"*

Will expressed, "You mean: Dad was broadcast to Earth and was replaced by…him?"

Penny yelled, "That's not dad?"

"My heavens, Jonathan! Where the hell are you?" Maureen semi-screamed and looked up.

Suddenly, the emotional, hot-blooded, Latin lover had enough and *violently reacted* to his new situation. Zorro backed up, grabbed his thin sword from its sheath, pulled it out, and yelled: "On guard!" He swished it in the air, to the left and right, in a horizontal '8' pattern. "This is madness! This is insane! I demand to know what this is!" He moved forward. There was fire in his angry eyes. He swished the sword again…

Doctor Smith casually walked in. But when he saw the Spanish character, he ran out and yelled: "He finally flipped his lid, he did!"

When the masked man in a cape stepped close to the others, *Robbie zapped Don Diego with an electric (taser) bolt*…and Zorro fell to the artificial floor, unconscious.

"Oh..my..God."

On Earth, John Robinson, in modern clothes, *simply appeared* in a small, sleepy, little, Mexican town. John was only seen by a drunk near the entrance of a saloon. After he came to his senses, John did not panic. He marched ahead and entered the saloon. The drunk on the ground waved, smiled and showed him his bad teeth.

Robinson instantly got the attention of everyone in the bar. Especially, a constable that *made time* with a waitress. He left her and went to where Jonathan was on the bar. "Do you have your papers, Amigo? Strangers must have papers. Let me see your papers."

"I, I don't have papers. I have nothing with me, sir."

"I see." The heavy-set policeman pulled out his thin sword and stuck it at John's neck. "Then, you have to come with me. No papers and a vagrant. This way." Mr. Robinson was soon locked in jail.

Onboard the Jupiter II, lost in space, the excitement settled down to a reasonable conversation between Don Diego [no mask], Will, his mother, and Robbie. Quite a bit was explained to the man from 1888.

"I had just finished a daring rescue of the lady Margurita Sanchez. I carried her back through her bedroom window. We were about to make love! That was when I heard a 'woosh' sound and suddenly I was on your ship. Ha, ha. And it's a ship that cannot find its way back home? Funny. I would have thought your machine-man would find the way, no?"

Robbie transmitted, *"It's complicated! Wormholes are involved!"*

"Wormholes?" Don Diego made a funny face.

Maureen laughed, "Ha, ha." She was charmed and overwhelmed by this man that appeared like Jonathan. He was dark and handsome; he was steamy and he was *ready to go!* She was extremely turned-on.

"I find you a beautiful woman, Maureen. You are as attractive as any lady I've ever known. And you are very, very, ah…intelligent…"

"Oh, stop it." Maureen smiled, giggled and waved her hand.

Will cringed slightly and then said, "Robot, I can't understand. I thought you'd lock onto an Earth object. I just found out you locked onto an old, fictional TV show…"

"So? What's the difference?" Robbie asked. *"Quanta in space."*

"SO? The transporter must have confused dad with his lookalike from the TV show. Logic says, if you're here, Don Diego, then my dad is in your TV world, or the situation where you come from."

"Really, Will?" Maureen said. "Then he might be alright?"

Don Diego exclaimed, "He is probably having a fine time! If he took my place, he just did a heroic act and could find himself in the arms of the beautiful Lady Margurita." Don winked at Will.

Maureen frowned and felt twinges of jealousy. She changed expression and asked her son: "Will? Is Jonathan coming back?"

The boy answered, "I'll do everything in my power, mom."

She nearly felt feverish (must be because of the cape). She said, "Take your time. I mean, I mean, I don't want anything to go wrong? Right…son?" Her eyes were glued on the swarthy Latino.

Back in 1988, in a dirty jail cell in Mexico…

Jonathan was having the time of his life because he was *fucking Lady Margurita!* The fabulously sexy and bodacious Lady Margurita with the wonderful brown eyes. The head of the police decided to execute the (American-looking) stranger at sunrise without a trial. But before that moment, he gave the accused one night of bliss with the damsel, formerly in distress. She was years younger than Maureen, well-skilled in the sexual arts and really 'hot to trot.' They fucked until early morning, when they heard the cocks that crowed<.

"That was awfully civil of the chief to give me a night with you."

Margurita was upset. She spit! She said, "Look what those peegs did to you, *shaved your mustache* that I love so much, and, and, what? They bleached your skin? How could they, Don?"

"I know! Those stinkin' bastards! Look what they did to me, not to mention the funny clothes they dressed me in, eh? *Is this really true,* Don will be executed at dawn? You mean they're serious?"

"Yes, my Don. But we have time. Put it in me again, my love…"

WHOOSH, and John suddenly materialized in bed with his wife. She was hot, sweaty and *screamed!* Then, calmed down when she realized what happened. The transference between John and Zorro was temporary. The two (Guy Williams) sprung back to their original universes. John had to explain his boner and the red lipstick all over his face and neck. Maureen had to explain a few things herself.

TS Caladan

The Robinsons onboard the Jupiter II discovered that the ship's energy had greatly been depleted so that another attempt to get a transporter that worked right would be impossible. John explained his encounter in the jail cell. He was very understanding when Maureen confessed to an affair with the caped and masked Zorro. Forgive and forget. The gang continued to be lost in space, but happy that they were together and whole again. "John? Could you grow a mustache?"

16 Sungate

IF the movie and television series called *Stargate* was Sungate, with basically the same characters, and they finally heard from Jack Tripper, who the SG-1 team thought had been dead for years!

Daniel, Samantha, T'lc and top brass at the underground Sungate complex were amazed, thrilled that their friend and comrade was not dead at the hands of Apophis, as reported years ago. An unexpected "in-coming" alerted the Sungate at the SG facility. Claxons blew; red lights flashed! Emergency-situation was called off when proper channels concluded the in-coming was safe. Then the "deadbolt" unscrewed on the Gate and the visitors or thing was allowed to arrive. After the usual, bright, psychedelic colors and patterns twirled like a spinning kaleidoscope in the center of the Circle...

Out popped a relatively small, metal canister. That was it. The colors and changing pattern stopped and faded away. The Gate closed.

When they opened the container, they found a hand-written note from Jack. The writing matched Tripper's. Jack wrote: *Friends, Colonel, you'll find this hard to believe. I barely believe it myself. Apophis did not kill me. He imprisoned me all this time in an odd world, a very/very odd world that is hard to describe. In fact, I'm still in jail! Still locked here and not sure how I'm getting' out. There is a Sungate in front of me that only I see. I can't beam out, but you could beam in. You see, our little alien friend, Hercules, found me. And the best he could do, because of energy expenditure, is send this note to you, not me or anything larger, see? It's fantastic, gang, if you really are reading this. I miss all of you guys. Even T'lc. Now, 'cos of the note, you now know the way here, can dial here and come get me. Once yer here the Gate should work normally and we'll all get back. You really won't believe my ah...prison? You gotta see this place, ha, ha. So, please, come as soon as you can and get me out of here!!*

The SG-1 team was so excited and anxious to collect their friend that they did not get a fourth. The main 3 were soon equipped and ready to go. They walked up the metal ramp and into the Sungate…

After all the intense colors, patterns and swirls…They came out of a Sungate on the other end, walked down a short ramp and soon saw Jack! He sat on a couch in a normal living room in New York. "Jack!" "There's Jack!" T'lc said: "He looks very comfortable."

Jack Tripper was not pleased to see the gang. He covered his face then got to his feet.

They ran to him, ready to explode with joy, when he sadly said: "You shouldn't have come. You shouldn't have believed the note…"

"Why not?" Daniel asked. They were all surprised at his words.

"Look," Jack said and pointed at the Sungate.

A *Deadbolt* materialized, turned and locked the Gate shut.

"Apophis planned this! To get the whole team here. For revenge. He waited. I been stuck in this madness for years, *Christ!"*

"Where's here?" Sam asked, as she looked around, wide-eyed.

Then, the front door opened with a *bang* and Chrissy and Janet, Jack's roommates, flew in and dashed off to their rooms. "We have to get stuff for the big party!" "Yeah, yeah. The Ropers will be there!"

Jack covered his face. "Oh, you don't know what it's been like."

The team looked at each other, oddly.

Sam said with a grin, "They look…cute. Ha, ha."

Jack explained, "When Apophis saw this television program with a character that had my name, he somehow got me trapped here, ha!"

"That's funny," Daniel said. They laughed, but were all trapped:

Until Hercules came along and saved the day. Because of SG-1's trip, he opened the Gate wider and brought the team home.

Jack didn't make the party.

TS Caladan

17 RATAVA

IF we could see the blue/green natives of Pandora 50 years after human contact, what would they be like? What would their jungle world appear like? This was not a future with corporations and companies mining the satellite for Unobtanium. It was a future where more and more Earthlings got in their chambers and assumed Avatar bodies, blue for jungle regions and turquoise for areas around water. How would modern people, rooted in technology and science, affect a planet of pure/innocent beings, based in the fundamentals of nature?

Fifty years after the first exploits of Jake Sulley and his family, Pandora has become a divided satellite. Today on Pandora, there were cities, small cities, in areas that were once jungles. Councils were created with full representation by natives. Nothing was constructed or mandated without full approval of the Na'vi natives. Over time, the blue or the blue-green youth became extremely fascinated with people. Everything our modern civilization offered, the Na'vi was interested in. Human ways enticed the large, intelligent and caring monkey-like creatures that they wanted to learn everything that they could about our society. The youth mimicked Earthlings, more and more; wore human clothes, listened to our music and did many of the activities that people did. The new movement was not respected or tolerated among a lot of tribe elders. Pandora stood very divided, with those who voted for jungle city constructions and the techniques of humans and those who remained very much opposed.

A computer class in a jungle city named Tara had just ended and three Na'vi students sat and spoke to each other at lunch. Each had on the latest fashions by Victoria's Secret. Old hits of Duran Duran were piped into the lunchroom. They enjoyed French fries, tacos and soda.

Aril told her two best friends, Zo and Orani, the big news: "You won't believe what the Na'vi science station has come up with, you simply won't, girls! My dad works there and I swear it's true! They now have chambers to fit us Pandorans…get this, we get in them, and we are shot through a warp-bridge all the fucking way to Earth! And, and we get *ratava* bodies, that's what they're calling them – we become human! Human, no tails. Pink, not blue! And smaller, right?"

"What?"

"Aril, I heard rumors of Pandoran chambers to Earth. You mean, it's true?"

Aril answered, "I know it's true because I'm

going…"

"What?!"

"Get out!"

"My dad's swinging it! Going to be *so cool!* Earth, in a ratava! Next week, I am gone! I'll tell you all about it…"

"You better," Zo said.

"Take pictures! We want to hear everything when you get back."

"You know I will. Can't wait!"

"Bitch."

"Ha, ha."

Over a "spaceways" channel, a dilation-free message was transmitted from Aril and received on Zo and Orani's phones. It read:

Not what I thought it would be. It's pretty rank here. Air is barely breathable, for me, anyway. And everything stinks. Hate this body. You'll appreciate how we relieve ourselves once you shit and piss like people. I had constant, never mind. Wait until you throw-up; that's a surprise. Now I know why so many of them came to our place to live. Funny, I had dreams of our blue world. Aaaah. Then I woke with all this shit around me, fuck! What the hell was I thinking? I miss my tail.

18 A Boy and his Cat*
(story by Daniel Hegel Jetson)

"You are really fucked up, man," Albert said to the cat. He found the cat outside of his cave in a stunned condition and he barely breathed. The good-looking, young man felt sorry for the calico cat with a gold diamond on his back, and carried him to his place, deeper in the cave. They came to his "home" with a fire and something like furniture. A rifle and strips of big bullets were up against a boulder. There were bottles of water in a niche in the rock.

"Here. Let's get a bit of food in you." Albert Swenson placed the cat gently on a pile of blankets. "It's not much, but it keeps me alive. It's called 'beef jerky.'"

"Seriously, you want me to eat beef jerky?" The kitty said [thoughts] out loud in English and it blew the mind of Albert.

"Wha…what? Did you say that?" the boy asked, astonishingly.

"You see anyone else here, brain boy?" the cat replied.

"That's, my God…that's *incredible!* Or am I out of my mind?"

"A little of both, aye? Alright. I was actually informed that I might be in link, or in sync, with one or two of you tall 2-leggers, that is, if I found one on the same frequency, wavelength? You know, in tune?"

"Huh? Can you tell me how I'm hearing you, puddy, and how it is you got this way? What, all cats use telepathy and can communicate with us, but they chose not to, until now? Is it the radiation?"

"That's just silly, Albert."

"You know my name?"

"I told you we're mentally-linked, didn't I? We're hooked, naturally, I think. Oh, how'd I get this way? No, all felines can't do this, nor would they want to do it. Listening in on all you crazy people. I'm actually old enough to remember a green world and *look what you did to it…*"

"It wasn't me, man."

"Yeah, yeah. Not you personally, but your kind. Look at the boat we're in now. It's a miracle anything survived the holocaust. Right?"

"You're telling me, kitty."

"My name's Eno and gimme the fucking jerky."

"Oh, ha. Sure." Albert grabbed a piece for himself and gave one to Eno. "Also, call me: Vic. That's what I wanna be called. Vic."

"You don't look like a Vic, Vic. I don't know. Maybe it's me?" [chewed the food]. "Mm, could be more tender."

"I'm a scavenger. That's how I've survived. I'm fast. I can hunt."

"I see. Cute. Not too smart. I think you need me to show you how to get a whole lot more in your life. What have you amassed? Some blankets, jerky and fire-sticks?"

"I don't need you, fucking talking-cat. What do I need you for? Another mouth to feed?"

"Huh. You said you hunt. I didn't explain what they did to me..."

"Who did what to you, Eno?"

"The freaking feds, connected to the war-effort. Everything, every lab experiment, seemed to be for the military. That was always the first thought: how can the government use the technology as a weapon? Anyhoo, they tested communicating with animals. Whales, dolphins. Dogs were way *too stupid*. It's a myth they're smart. You don't really want to talk to a dog. Cats were ideal because we're brilliant, free-range; we can slink into houses and be so darn loveable, aye? They thought they could talk to us by enhancing us. *I'm enhanced, baby!*"

"Explain, please."

"My senses have been permanently stimulated, like tripping on LSD. We cats already were tripping, compared to you guys. But the lab cats they fiddled with, like me, we're *really fucking tripping balls*, you know what I mean, Vic?"

"No. But I have to look at it from a practical sense, yes? You haven't explained exactly what you can do for me; why I need you?"

"Here it is, and think about this, my friend. All my sensations are ten times what they were and cats are almost like birds. I can track anything and SEE for you when you, when we, scavenge around..."

"I don't buy it," Vic said, coldly.

"I can SMELL, smell 100 times better than you, Brainiac! I'll be your scout-cat; I'll earn my keep on our first mission."

"I don't know. What can you find better than a dog?"

Eno thought and changed tactics. "I can find pussy."

"Why would I want more cats?"

"No, you jerk! Pussy! Vaginas! Whohas. Twats. Cunts. Chicks. Women. Babes! You're a handsome boy, surely, you've used your looks to get what you want?"

"Yes."

"You fuck girls, don't you?"

"I love fucking girls!"

"Yeah, I knew that. Hey. Come here." Eno wasn't as hurt as he let on and dashed toward the entrance of the cave. When he was outside, he put his front paws on a rock and got as high as he could. Almost an endless, flat desert stretched in every direction. It was hot, dry and very sunny. "Sss, sss, sss," the cat smelled the air and then got a direct bead on... "Women! There, in that precise direction. The journey will take hours, but it might be well worth the trip, my friend? You're stocked on jerky. How's about a little fun? That direction, Vic."

Albert Swenson [Vic] said, "I think yer snowin' me good, buddy. And just want to team up with me so I take care of you. But, alright. I could use some adventure. We'll see where it leads us, pal."

"Now, you're talking. Let's get your stuff together and go, go!"

Vic made sure not to forget his rifle and ammo. That direction led to a lame cantina that did not provide much for survivors: A roof over their heads, gruel (barely edible), dirty water, some type of semi-safe ale, but most of all: whores! The backrooms were for prostitutes and their johns. No money system. Every barroom purchase and backroom transaction was conducted on a barter system: trade, material things that have been found from the old world that might have value.

Vic was never in this place before. As soon as he

entered, he got the layout of the survivor's "café." He received wanton looks from a few of the girls. A big smile crossed his face. "Maybe I'll keep you around for a while, cat."

"Heh, heh, sssss, yes. I think we found a pussy jackpot!"

Vic asked the proprietor, "Is he Okay? He's fine. He's with me." Eno found a comfortable place on Vic's shoulders.

"Sure. I like cats. They're rare now. First one is on the house, and 'course, feel free to go in the back at your leisure, sir. But maybe you should check the gun with me?" He left a drink and served others.

Vic left the gun and strips of bullets. He was excited to explore the backroom and he finished the swill quickly.

Eno asked, "What do you have to trade, boss?"

Vic thought the guy next to him at the bar heard the cat's words, looked at him and "Not so loud" came out of his mouth.

"I didn't know I was loud, young man. I'll watch that, aye?"

"No, hey man, remember, only someone on our wavelength can hear my thoughts. They can't."

"I see."

"Okay." The man moved a few seats down from Vic.

"Here's what I have to trade." Vic opened a large zipper and showed him many small bottles of "Penicillin, it's called. Stops any infection. It's better than anything tradeable. What a place this is, eh?"

"Mmmm. Dude, can't you smell all the pussy?"

"You know, E. I think I can. Why am I waiting? Let's go."

In the back, he could have chosen any curtain. Vic chose the first one and pushed his way inside. There he met Billy Jean. She was a redhead (that looked a lot like Melanie Griffith). Sexy, beautiful body and hardly any clothes. They instantly fell for each other. Billy Jean never saw a guy after the holocaust that looked anything like Vic. She wanted so much more than just a fuck. Her mind worked overtime~.

Eno watched the love-making. After a furious fuck that lasted an hour, she believed she found her mate and said, "Look. Vic. I'm really a spy for the underground…"

"There's an underground?"

"Ha, ah. Yeah, there's an underground. Where you been?"

The boy shrugged. He looked at the cat. Eno didn't know.

"Underground?"

"Did you hear anything?"

"No," she replied. She couldn't hear the cat.

Billy Jean kissed him again. She was happy and in love. I swear we could take over New Topeka, my darling…"

"New Topeka?"

"That's what we call the settlement we've built underground. It is quite extensive with modern conveniences that don't exist here on the surface. You must come with me and see it. But it is a big secret, you understand?"

"Yes, Billy Jean. I'd love to see and experience modern things that I've only heard about or seen pictures of. Yes, let's go! But what do you mean we can take over the settlement?"

"Sure, we can. I'm like a princess there because my father runs a committee of three people and they make all the rules. Of course, we can take over and run the city like a King and Queen! That is, once you kill my father and the other two."

"Huh? You said kill your father?"

Later, she took Vic and Eno to a weird structure way out in the desert. They were miles from the closest person. It appeared like a very thick tree trunk with stunted branches on top. Gray striations lined the bark. You could barely see the impression of a door. Billy Jean knew exactly where to press to open the automatic elevator down to the underground and New Topeka.

He grabbed her shoulders, looked into her green eyes, fluffed her red hair and smiled. "Before we go, I have to say something to my cat in private. You understand?"

"Ha, ha. Sure, go ahead, Vic."

The boy took the cat to the other side of the structure. He heard his good buddy with four legs that said:

"Don't go, Vic."

"What? Good food, showers, electricity, modern conveniences, she said. Why wouldn't I want that? And I get *her;* she's beautiful and I could be king of the whole place? What the fuck? Why not go??"

Eno answered, "Have I ever steered you wrong, buddy?"

Vic said, "You only steered me here, cat."

"I'm speaking from my enhanced heart. I love you, you big dummy. She does not. I didn't like her from the start..."

"Why not?" Vic asked.

"Try thinking without your pecker. Doesn't it seem a little fishy? You really going to kill her father and take control of the kingdom? You really don't sense you're falling into a trap? I do. Sap. Don't go."

"I'm sorry. Look, I'll leave the gun and ammo here. No, I'm not going to kill no one. But I gotta go and see what they have. It's the scavenger in me. Come. Eno the cat, let's check out New Topeka together, all of us. C'mon."

"I'm staying right here. That's what my heart tells me to do. And, big guy, I'm pretty smart.

You're going to be very sorry, my friend."

"Bye." Vic waved and was sad. Heartbroken, actually. When he went to the other side of the tree-thing, she had the door open. He walked in and *they plunged all the way down to the underground.*

Once down on the bottom level, there was darkness and they heard music. Band music, patriotic music. Lights at the end of a tunnel showed them where to go. In no time, they made it to New Topeka. It appeared very strange: marching bands, graveyards, orchestras and people in old-fashion clothes that lined the streets. Traditional, wooden buildings from an earlier era. Lights illuminated certain sections. The black background was a constant reminder this was very much an underground facility that only resembled a quaint, old town.

"I know where to go to get our masks."

"What do you mean masks, Billy?"

"It's the rules, funny rules he and his damn committee impose upon all of us. Why do you think I want to end his fucked-up reign. This is perfect. You'll see what I mean in a minute, Vic."

They covered their faces and made it to the main church. No one saw that they weren't wearing masks. Next to the front door was a container with masks (if anyone had an old/damaged one, here were replacements). They put them on. The masks appeared like the faces of clowns. She directed him to the front door and they went in…

The prime church was where justice was dispensed. There were only a few people in the seats and they all had their clown masks on. At the front, elevated section, stood Roboss, her father and the two other members of the committee, one male and one female. They wore no masks, yet they imposed mandates that *all must wear them.*

She said, "Keep watching, listening, Vic. I know it'll be bad."

Vic saw a large man dressed in clothes a farmer would wear. He stood very tall behind the three sitting committee members.

"Who's he?"

She replied, "That's the STN Killer Robot programmed to be 100% loyal to my father. He's the enforcer. There are only 2 penalties for crimes in New Topeka: you're sent to the farm and work for a year at hard labor or you're eliminated by the STN. ...Look, criminals."

A man and woman were brought in front of the committee by the STN and thrown to the floor!

Roboss stated, "You have been found of no recent crime, just a general disregard for our authority. You've been seen twice without your masks on. Both of you. So, your sentence will be...*death...*"

"Lord, Roboss!" the man yelled. "We have done no mortal crime! We are willing to work at the farm. Surely, we've only committed a minor crime, one that warrants a year punishment, certainly no more. Roboss, please, you must listen to reason for the sake of my wife, sir."

Billy Jean's father calmly said, "You are correct. You and your wife have committed no major crime. No one has in the longest time. You see, we have to make an example of you, so people do not forget our power and that they must obey what we say without question." He motioned to the STN, a slice-action to the neck. They were taken in back to be killed.

"Nooooo!" "Please, reconsider, sir. We'll work for

10 years!"

Vic said to Billy: "I've seen enough. This is insane. What's left of the human race down here is pure madness. I have to get out." Vic left and Billy followed.

When they were outside, she said. "Wait, here. I know where I can get a gun." Billy Jean ran off wildly in a direction where a black background was all around her.

Vic wandered aimlessly and avoided a few of the insane clown-people. He heard the Star-Spangled Banner played. There were recorded sounds that suggested: 'hints for the day.' This was a bizarre programmed society and Albert "Vic" Swenson wanted out of it. He desired the surface world, desperately. He wanted to be with Eno, not this crazy woman who wanted to reign as Queen.

Billy returned with a gun and gave it to Vic. She said, "Now when the committee comes out, shoot them dead!"

He held onto the pistol in the middle of the street. He decided: He was not going to kill anyone. Both of them took off their masks.

The committee didn't come out, the STN Killer Robot in farmer's clothes came out! "Aargh!" The big android attacked the girl and boy! They barely got away from its grip.

He shot the pistol at it, but the caliber was so small that it did no damage to the robot. Vic threw the gun away. The race was on! "This way! Back the way we came!"

They ran through main street, passed the marching bands, the graveyard and the patriotic music.

The Killer Robot was not far behind and programmed to kill them.

They reached the dark tunnel system and the automatic elevator. It took them to the surface where Billy and Vic saw Eno through the door. The cat faithfully waited for his boy to return.

"Big lug. I knew you'd be back."

"Yeah, but we're being chased!" They remembered who was behind them and jumped out of the door on the gray, striated tree.

Another cage brought the next one, which was the Killer Robot. "Aaaargh." It screamed and was about to crush the boy and girl…

But Vic used his high-powered rifle and shot 40 big bullets into its face and chest and put the thing out of operation in seconds! It fell to the desert floor, a useless hunk of metal.

"Vic! Fantastic! This is perfect! There is nothing that can stop us now. Committee without its enforcer is nothing! Your big gun tops anything we have below. Now, let's go down and rule as royalty…"

Vic's smile turned to a frown. He said, "No way, honey. I want no part of the madness below. You be queen. I won't be king, babe."

She was angry. Without words, she turned and went below.

Vic was so happy. He was with Eno, his cat! "I love you, boy!"

"So, you finally came to your senses? I told you: *you need me.* I tried to steer you away from her, remember? But no, no, you had to learn the *hard way.* I love you too, man. I smell sausages. *Really.* Sausages. That way."

"Ha, ha."

19 The Pittsburgh Experiment

IF the Philadelphia Experiment and the unbelievable events at Montauk, NY, happened differently, and occurred within a restricted, military shipyard on the Monongahela River.

In 1943, at the height of WWII, the secret Pittsburgh Project neared completion. The goal of the experiment was to render our destroyers and battleships *invisible* to enemy radar screens. In this way, our Navy's warships could sneak up on enemy targets without being seen until the final moments of the attack.

'The Pittsburgh Experiment,' as it was later called, was a project created by (alien from Venus, who was born in space) Nikola Tesla. Because of George Westinghouse, Tesla had many connections to Pittsburgh. The project was his conception and he also co-funded it. The great inventor was positive he could "beam" a warship, specifically the U.S.S. Cleaver, out of the Monongahela River and all the way to the Atlantic Ocean, to the Montauk station's shipyard! This was NOT what the U.S. and Britain wanted; they did not want a warship with lightspeed capabilities and a full spectrum of problems starting and stopping, which *broke the normal laws of time and space!* The feds and royal scientists only wanted a ship that cloaked itself and became invisible to enemy eyes and their radar screens.

If Tesla remained on the project, the military would have had perfected destroyers and battleships with lightspeed capabilities that constantly vibrated, which made them invisible. And they could attack, even behind a *wall of invisibility.* Tesla was given the problem, and solved it, but in a far more cosmic way than military leaders and the best scientists could ever imagine.

The Military Industrial Complex, headed by the Throne of England, *refused Tesla's concept* and called it: "Theoretical nonsense" and "Way-out" and "It will never work." The statements were from the most prestigious, scientific minds of the time. Tesla walked off the project and made one of the fewest mistakes he ever made in his life: He did not destroy all of the groundwork, the paperwork, from the project. Usually, Nick worked out everything in his head. But the physics and the numbers were much too critical in this case and the math had to be worked out perfectly in advance.

Tesla had a lot more on his mind than the crazy war at the time and the Project. He planned to escape the planet. Not by a personal saucer (which was possible), but by Vortex (like a Stargate). He never thought England would go ahead with the Pittsburgh Project and turn it into what they had intended from the start: a cloaked warship, to simply make it invisible.

Nils Bohr, Townsend Browne, Albert Einstein and Al Bielek were called in on the project, the most intelligent men the government knew. They were given the assignment: *See what can be gleaned from Tesla's notes and make it work, make the U.S.S. Cleaver invisible!*

They tried, and something terrible went wrong and endangered the lives of the soldiers aboard the Cleaver because of all the electrical and magnetic power the experiment generated and needed to succeed!

Too much power built-up and like feedback over speakers, the energy MAGNIFIED to such a point that...

A hard, black SPHERE of an inert material appeared around the destroyer. A very loud and forceful, EM phenomenon turned the river into black glass around the destroyer. Smoke was everywhere under a very black and starless sky. Viewers observed an atmosphere that appeared unreal or surreal. *Something definitely went wrong!*

Hours passed. Officials and scientists were not clear on exactly what to do next? Then, the hard/black material that encased the ship eventually dissolved to nothingness~. It was gone. The ship was there, but in what shape was the crew?

TS Caladan

Twelve people were taken to the secret McKeesport underground facility. Strangely, Al Bielek and his brother Duncan, who worked the control room, were missing. A few others of the 18 crew members went missing, seemingly vanished into thin air and were presumed dead. The 12, known as the "McKeesport Boys," were studied by federal scientists, under British authority. Technicians and doctors discovered bizarre oddities among the 12:

Each was traumatized, physically/mentally, by the Event. The strangest abnormality was the fact that *four of the boys disappeared and then reappeared in different places!* They had no idea where they vanished. They were here, and then suddenly they were in a different place. Five of the boys felt very sick; they held no food down and threw-up again and again. Three of the boys were unconscious and badly burned by radiation. The nine conscious boys felt the same way: Like they were not there, like they *didn't* or *shouldn't* exist in this reality. It was difficult for them to hold onto reality, as if they lost their own material integrity. They complained of severe headaches. There was nothing the doctors and technicians could do to help them.

Each of the McKeesport Boys, in their own time, *disappeared!* It was as if they were only ghost-images of their true selves, which they split from because of the Event. The incident on the Pittsburgh river was covered up for decades and only recently has the truth been realized. The U.S.S. Cleaver was towed to the Montauk shipyard in New York and studied.

The story does not end there. Al Bielek and his brother, Duncan, onboard the Cleaver were projected into the future by the Event. They spent a considerable time there. In a very advanced medical facility, they were treated for radiation burns and quickly healed. But the Event still had a grip on them...

They were returned to the 20th Century and lived long lives. They told their fantastic story and few people believed them. A film called *The Pittsburgh Experiment* made it to theaters and the recreation was very close to true events (minus the love story Hollywood added). In the public's mind, this was a piece of fiction. But insiders knew differently. Al and Duncan were a part of a secret government think-tank of geniuses and super-geniuses long before the Event. But who in modern times took them seriously after the Event? Their tales of aliens and Lizard-people who worked with our governments, vortexes that transported people to other times and other places like Stargates, that Al's brother Duncan was de-aged, suddenly decades younger than he should have been, and Al, who was rebirthed into a whole other life...who would believe such incredible stories? You might not if the claims came from just anyone. These were the smartest people on the planet and that's why their advice and wisdom were essential to feds.

Brother Duncan really had a special mind with advanced psi-abilities that was tested by the machines at McKeesport, over and over. If you said "apple" to Duncan (Cameron), a real/physical apple would miraculously appear in the test lab. If you created a "mental vortex" between the present year and another year...in other words, if Duncan was told it and pictured it in his mind...*it would be true*. Test subjects actually traveled from one time to another like a Time Machine because of this oddity from one of the McKeesport Boys!

A very dangerous incident happened via Duncan's

FEARS. A Monster was made, materialized at Pittsburgh's facility and ran amok! It was a hunkering, savage, tall and powerful brute out of Duncan's ID, like in the movie 'Forbidden Planet.' A real beast was crystallized from a *mind* and did a lot of physical damage to the underground lab. Then, they cut the power plug and creature dissolved, never returned.

Al Beliek often lectured with Duncan and Preston Nichols (also highly used by the government for his mind) and made cheap videos that could be seen on YouTube. Insiders are well-aware of the amazing events because of the Pittsburgh Experiment. Outsiders do not have a clue.

20 Day of the Dead Living

IF the dead rose from their graves, only there was an odd switch to the familiar story.

Sorry to report that on this particular parallel Earth, the white men have been canceled out to a point of extinction. Every year, there were less and less white people. Factors that accounted for this:

*White people were discriminated against because of "Black Privilege."

*White people were not hired for jobs.

*White people no longer received scholarships.

*White people were thought of as contagious and the carriers of deadly viruses.

*Black people married black people and no longer mixed races.

The result over many years was the elimination of "whitey." White people could no longer provide for their families. Caucasians were a dying group of people.

Whites became the minority and the homeless. They were no longer seen in movies, on TV or in ads. Whites were gone from social media and from the streets.

Cities contained all blacks, in time.

And, no one seemed to care?

Mother Nature cared. Maybe it was a twisted Mother Nature, but that Twisted Sister found a way and fought back…

The "phenomenon" was first noticed when Ben Johnson from Alliquippa, PA. visited the Oakmont Cemetery where his parents were laid to rest. He had a dozen roses that he always placed down at their stones this time of year, 6 for mother and 6 for father.

Suddenly, about 60 feet away, the man noticed an oddity: It appeared as if a very pale black man attacked a young lady!? He grabbed her violently and she fought back! Ben jumped to the lady's rescue. He ran to her and saw that it was not a pale black man – it was a *white guy!* A really fucked-up white guy. *But they were all dead? What was a white guy doing walking around?* "Hey! Let 'er go!!" Ben Johnson yelled at the zombie-like creature that moved really weird.

"Help me!" she screamed.

The white "thing" went to bite the girl.

But Ben laid a big punch on the creature, right on the button and *broke his face.* It came apart. The white man appeared to have crawled out of his grave with ripped clothes and ripped, bloodless skin. It laid on the ground and gyrated a bit, but seemed to be *out of commission* and could not get up.

"Are you alright, Miss? Are you hurt?"

"I, I think I'm fine. It grabbed me, but I'm not cut.

It's awful! It was a white man!" she said filled with fear.

"I can see that, miss. I sure will report it to the authorities. I'm Ben…"

"I'm Alicia, and, and thank you, Ben."

"It looks dead, that's funny…or very low on energy. I think…"

Ben noticed 2 other figures among the headstones They did not walk normally and their skin was not very black. "We better go. Will you come with me and report this also? They'll never believe me."

Alicia replied, "Of course, Ben. Let's go."

Later, that same day, Arsenio Hall, host of NBC's 'Chiller Theater,' had mic in hand and now hosted a quasi-news-documentary from the Oakmont Cemetery. He said to the black cameraman:

"Yes, friends, this is no joke. I have an exclusive, but very soon federal scientists will be here to figure out how this could have happened, but…*it seems*…the dead have come to life. There have been 4 cases of it, whatever it is, from this graveyard, and these creatures are in a mindless state…and each of the 4 cases have been male men who are Caucasian. Yes. Authorities have no clue what could have caused this, this, *animation* of the dead…or why this has only affected the white dead? Are mysteries. I can tell you, the 'phenomenon,' it's been called, will be dealt with by federal officials and there is no reason to panic. I, ah, what was that, Lou?"

The cameraman pointed at what came over a small hill.

Arsenio was shaken and said, "Let's get the hell out of here!"

An incident occurred aboard Trans World Airlines, flight 103, out of Rome. The story was the last white man in Italy was a tourist and had previously arranged for his body to be buried in LA, his home. But international laws only recently allowed Chet Backowski's body to be returned to the states. Coming into Los Angeles, from the storage compartment in the plane, dead Chet rose up out of his coffin. He walked through the aisle and 'terrorized' all of the black people onboard. It was not clear if they were terrified because he was a dead man come back to life…or that he was a white man?

In the next days, more and more of the white dead got out of their caskets and crawled to the surface. Especially around the area of the Oakmont Cemetery, where the phenomenon seems to have originated. Now a number of cases have been reported in most countries. The creepy zombies were all male. Were they the last traces of those who once ruled the world? Did the Whiteman zombies want revenge and want their world back?

One news report over Media channels stated: "We are under attack by the dead. Various reasons have been offered as to the cause of the phenomenon, but there has been nothing conclusive found so far. They can be killed or stopped by shotguns that target their cerebral cortex. We can only advise you to barricade yourself in defensible places like basements, get supplies, and arm yourself. The National Guard has been called to the Pittsburgh area, where the contagion seems the most concentrated. But the attacks have also been reported in all major cities. Do not panic, please, and we will all get through this. Stay tuned for more reports with the latest updates…"

On the way to the authorities, Alicia and Ben were blocked on a side road by the zombies! They piled enough rocks that made the road impassable. They attacked from the side! This forced Ben and Alicia to run! The couple were fast and outran their attackers. They found what they thought was an abandoned house. When they searched the basement, they saw an unusual scene they never expected:

A young man who introduced himself as "Tyrese" had one of the white zombies tied to a pole. It was a very recent dead zombie and in good shape. In fact, IT TALKED.

"Have you forgotten?" the Walking Dead said. "You were brought to this country as SLAVES! Now, you seek vengeance and you rule! It's Okay to destroy the white man because of what their great, great grandfathers had done? No, it's not. You acted as the worst slave-masters near the end. Your fucking rap music will never go away! It's shit and it's everywhere! All black shows and movies, huh? What is television now, local shows from Selma, Alabama? No shit *Black Lives Matter,* much, much more than white! Look what you've done to us, to the white man! You killed us!! Your great leaders like Doctor Martin Luther King fought for EQUAL rights, not *Superior* rights! Even he would recognize what you fucking did to Whitey? And condemn it! Anyone from the past would look at the world today and condemn it! Look at you bald, bastard, bearded SLAVES when hair has always meant strength, vitality and most of all: FREEDOM! Covered in stupid tattoos of Slavery! You addicted, sleeping/woke people, addicted to your damn phones today. You are EMPTY! You know nothing of what you're doing or should be doing because you are so into *social media of nonsense* and your *goddamn phones,* which have taken over your lives and are very, very dangerous in the long run. But you've been dumbed-down so much, you're idiots and DO NOT CARE about what you should be caring about, and what you should be doing. You are heartless, cold cogs of the A.I. Machine now. You're the machine! You're the Walking Dead, not me!! YOU ARE THE MINDLESS ZOMBIES, NOT ME!!"

Suddenly, outside, a black man had heard enough and shot his shotgun through an open window. On target. Zombie was stopped.

"Enough of that shit," the gunman said. Tyrese agreed.

Ben and Alicia had frightened expressions and were not sure.

21 The Mirror of Dorian White

What IF identical twin brothers were abandoned at birth and lived separate lives, then met for the first time on a train and discovered that there was a myriad of parallels between the two?

Dorian White was a normal type of Londoner in the year 1905, youthful, handsome and fairly rich. He rode First Class on a train from New Kensington to Brighton. His purpose was to surprise a cousin he'd not visited in quite some time near Brighton Beach. The porter had punched Dorian's ticket just before a very bizarre occurrence:

A man walked into the same First-Class

compartment on the train, which was reserved for only two passengers and startled Dorian. "Blimey. Can't be. The man in the mirror?" Dorian whispered to himself when the man entered. The stranger was also shocked to see Dorian. The oddities that confronted the men were 1) they wore very similar, stylish clothes and 2) *they had almost the same face!* Dorian appeared younger, more attractive with a clean/shaven face. The man who walked into the compartment had a scruffy beard, marks on his face and looked as if he was Dorian's brother. In fact, he was.

They introduced each other and were further surprised because they had the same first name: Dorian. That was strange enough, but they were more stunned at their last names: White and Black. The man who appeared older was Dorian Black. Amazing, what were the odds? More incredible similarities were realized once the men spoke at length. Each had mothers that had abandoned them and they soon realized: *they had the same mother!* When this moment happened, the Dorians hugged and cried in each other's arms. Both men always wanted siblings, and now they had found their long-lost brother. The parallels or mysteries did not end there. Each discovered that they had the same birthday, on the same year! But how could that be when Dorian Black looked more advanced in years than Dorian White?

Dorian White invited Mr. Black to his home in New Kensington for dinner at a later date. Dorian Black accepted. The boys were excited and had to learn more of the other. White thought, *did my twin have a hard, cruel, tortured life? Was that why he appeared haggard and older?*

Mr. Black was met by a butler when he knocked on the door of Mr. White's splendid residence. "Please come in, sir." The house appeared very old, but was maintained well. Everything was clean, polished and dusted. Sculptures were in appropriate places, beautiful artwork hung on walls. Thick, immaculate carpets. Candles provided lighting. White's home was impressive and familiar to Mister Black.

White told Avery, the butler, he could leave and was not needed.

"Strange, but true, my new brother," Black said to White.

"What's that, Dorian?"

"Ha, ha. My house is eerily similar. Oh, my. Only I have no manservant and I've let the place fall to near ruin, I'm afraid. I, I, dear brother, have not been successful in life. Failed businesses, mostly. Crooked partners. You can imagine how cutthroat business dealings can get, aye? I shouldn't have purchased First Class, but I've always wanted to. You see, I'm in the same clothes, the only good clothes I own. I've had to sell a lot of items I've inherited from the Blacks…"

"Brother, if you need a loan? I would be happy to help you," White said in earnest. "My foster parents left me with a bundle…"

Black Dorian smiled, showed a few missing teeth, and said, "I may take you up on that, brother. Good to know. Thank you."

"No problem at all. Come this way. You have to see this." The men got up and walked into another large room.

"Oddly similar, I must say," Black expressed.

"Here it is, brother." White lifted his arm and walked

close to an old mirror with a wooden frame that appeared out of the Dark Ages, medieval. It was clean, but worn and showed its age. The design of the frame could go back to the *first mirrors of royalty*. Its angle was tilted so that Black did not view his image. White saw into it. He stood there in absolute amazement as his head turned from the mirror to Black, and then back again. "Extraordinary!"

"What is it, my good man?" Black acted cool, as if this was all news to him.

"Stand right there, Dorian." White was delighted, intrigued and very confused. "We've shared a few intimate stories, brother. I feel I can trust you. What I am about to share with you now, I have not told a soul. It's been years, and I've told no one." His eyes enlarged.

"You have my attention, brother."

White said, "The White family that raised me were, how can I say it? Witches…"

"Witches?" Black echoed his brother's word.

"Good witches, I can assure you. Ha, ha. 'White witches' is the term and they chose that for a surname. Ancient bloodlines. There are a lot of odd items in this house, in the attic, that I'm sure people who collect antiques would pay a fortune for."

"That's funny, brother. I inherited a posh-load of statues and old paintings as well. Unfortunately, I had to sell them over the years. Valuable items I once owned…are now gone. Bizarre parallels, eh?"

"This mirror was one of the items mother brought down from the attic. She told me strange tales about it; that it would protect me, keep me extremely viral and healthy, keep me safe from harm. And other things that she didn't tell me at the time, but said I would eventually find out. Mother said it was 'enchanted.'"

"Enchanted? Ha, ha." Black smiled. He was in good spirits and enjoyed every word from his brother.

"Alright. Okay," White directed Black to: "Now, come here and stand next to me. We'll look into the mirror together, aye?" His hand motioned for Black to come.

Black Dorian walked up to his brother and stood shoulder-to-shoulder with him. They peered into the glass together and...

"Ah, ah...brother Dorian? I, I see nothing funny or peculiar, ah, whatsoever. To the left is me and my rough exterior, I've had a 'ard life, you see, sir? On the right is you in your fine clothes who appears like my young brother, my rich, good-looking, younger brother..."

"You do not see one image?!"

"Wacha mean, sir, one? There are two of us."

"Yes, yes, I know," White said with a dazed look in his eyes. "I expected to see two, too. But, Mr. Black, I assure you on my family's good name, I see one man in the mirror *and that man is you!*"

"Me?!"

"Yes, yes. As soon as I saw you on the train, it was as if my reflection walked into the car! My expression was beyond simply seeing a lost twin brother, or it should have been?"

"Dorian? You just told me the mirror's enchanted...?"

"Right."

"Well, that's it man! I don't believe in such things, *but you do.* You are making yourself see odd things in it, if you believe it to be magic? Sounds psychological."

"Could that be it? Dorian White rubbed his chin and

took another gander at the mirror's reflection. There was just one man, alone, and his reflective image was of Mr. Black. "It is extraordinary."

Black asked, "What else did your mother tell you about it?"

"She said it will speak the truth, but I don't know what that means. It's never spoken to me, so far, as far as I know. I guess you don't have an enchanted mirror at your residence, do you, Mr. Black? That would…"

Black burst with laughter, very loud. "HA! Ha! Haaaa! It would be another coincidence! But no, Mr. White. I have no magic mirror. Although, I could have sold a similar mirror long ago. I'm not sure. What does your butler see when he looks into it?"

"He sees a normal reflection. Like you do. Apparently, the mirror is meant for me. I must be as enchanted as the glass, ha."

Black replied, "Maybe you are, sir? Maybe the witches that raised you put a spell on both you and the mirror? No?"

"Dorian, that would explain my connection to it; we're bonded. You know our age. Look at me and tell me how old do I appear?"

Black answered: "Both of us are 40 years old, yet you look like a strong, fit man of *20 years*. I, on the other hand, appear near 60, to, to the view of others. Dorian? Are you saying the old mirror has kept you young?!"

"That's it, brother. Magic Mirror of my family has kept me free from disease and sickness, I believe. Ha, and kept me from *ageing*. I haven't aged since I first saw the enchanted mirror twenty years ago. I haven't been sick, or busted a toe or lost a drop of blood since then. There's more. Twice, I've been thrown by my horse, high in the air! Both times, there just happened to be a bale of hay in the perfect spot to break my fall. Was it the mirror's doing? I think it's my good luck charm, given me great luck, in fact! My businesses are very profitable, ha. When I bet on the horses, *I win!* Do I thank the magic mirror?"

Dorian Black touched its old wooden frame and said, "This is exactly what I need, a good-luck hex, a positive charm or talisman that'll make me happy in life, rich. Yet, brother, *you see my reflection in it?* How very strange? As if it foretold of our meeting? Could be?"

"I don't know, sir. Time will tell. Now! Let's have some of my best brandy? I'll pour."

"Aye! That sounds very reasonable, ha, ha. I envy you very much, my brother."

"Yes. I've been very, very...*lucky,*" White said as he saw himself in the mirror, an old man with a rough beard. He took a moment and wondered about the things that were revealed in the conversation.

It was much later that evening. Black had gone home. White was up and could not get to sleep. He got up and drank more brandy. He made his way in front of the enchanted mirror and pulled up a seat. He sat and so did the man with a beard with marks on his face. The reflection was not Mister Black. It was another entity and it *spoke,* the mirror finally spoke. It said, "Dorian, this is Elsbeth, the mother who raised you. Ha, I'm sure this is very peculiar: my words coming from your brother's image, but you remember my voice, yes?"

"It *is* you, mother! It is your voice. I'm, I'm..."

"Don't get emotional, son. You look well. A little drunk, but you look well..."

"Ha, ha. I'm fine. What is it you want to tell me?"

"Your brother means to *kill you!* He was raised by a rival house of ours, the Blacks…"

"Rival witches, you mean, mother?"

"Yes. Specifically, our enemy coven. His family did not love him like we love you, son. It was basic torture. As a means of punishment for any small crime or indiscretion, he was given an ancient mirror, this mirror's negative twin. Whenever he misbehaved, he'd age, and not age well. For lies, for thievery, for any mean prank that all children are guilty of, Dorian paid the price: He aged; his skin grew sores, he wrinkled, while all the time, his reflection remained young. Can you see the madness such cruel witchcraft would spark and fester inside him? Then…*you appeared.* You are his reflection come to life! His beautiful, young, identical-twin brother. You are everything he is not and could have been. Believe me, my son, he will attempt to kill you; I don't know how or when. But be very careful, my sweet son…"

"I love you so much, mother." Dorian's eyes dropped. He was sleepy.

"Go to bed, Dorian."

"Yes, mother."

There was a sharp contrast of circumstances at the empty, dirty, dark and dreary estate of the Black Family. Dorian held a candelabra in his right hand and was prepared to throw it into his mirror and break it into little pieces! *"Tell me why I shouldn't do it, father!!"*

The reflection was the clean-shaven, young, viral and healthy version of Dorian…only it was a very dark spirit and not Mr. White. It spoke. It said: "You need me to tell you the next step and *all the steps after that,* my son! You know of your curse! You need me to help you fend off the next crisis you are fated to encounter. *Son, please!"*

"NO!" The bearded, real Dorian screamed, then screamed again: "I know what to do!!" He tossed the candelabra into the ancient mirror and it SHATTERED. The evil, enchanted mirror of warlocks *died.*

The next day, Dorian Black found out how to get to the rear of White's estate, where there were stables and a horse track. He knew that his brother rode in the afternoons. He set up a rifle on small legs and he waited.

His brother appeared and was alone. Minutes later, after one lap of the track, White stopped and became the perfect target. Crosshairs were placed on the image of his head and *a bullet was placed through his brain!* White was murdered by Mister Black.

Black had opened a bathroom window latch a day before when he was at White's home. He hoped it stayed unlatched. From the backyard, Dorian opened the window and crawled into the house. He found the Lucky Mirror and stood with his back toward it.

Black's intentions were clear. He desired all the possessions of his brother. In their talks he learned, Dorian White had very few friends, only a cousin that barely stayed in touch. His brother lived his life as a virtual hermit locked up in the mansion. Black wanted to get his hands on the treasures that he knew laid in the attic. A goldmine of antiques worth a fortune! *"His business empire is mine now!"*

The enchanted mirror, the mirror of incredible luck and fortune to brother White, *should shine on me now,*

Black thought. All roads led here. Mr. White was dead, there was no doubt about that. "I'm his closest kin! Our blood is the same! This is my inheritance! They cannot prove I shot my brother! It's all mine now. Mine, mine, mine!" he shouted. Then he turned and faced the mirror…

And saw…

An exact duplicate of himself. Not a young, clean, fresh version. Dorian observed a reverse reflection, like any normal mirror. The image in the mirror was a man over 60 years old who was withered, weak, thin, with a pocked face and sores on his skin. He had a very unattractive beard. The image spoke to Dorian and said:

"Brother! Don't you recognize me?"

"Mister White? Is that you?" Black knew it was and shook to the marrow of his bones. The enchanted mirror was bonded to White and now contained his spirit.

"You thought I was dead? Ha, ha. Hell, I thought I was dead, too. Then I came back. Back here. Now, *I see you*. I see you very well and I know you think you've won, but you haven't won a damn thing!"

"Oh, no?? You think I haven't won?" Black ran to a fireplace and grabbed one of the pokers. Before he ran back to smash the mirror…

The Magic Mirror switched the Dorians! The old, bearded Dorian was the reflection and the young, shaven one lived and breathed in the real world. White took a few moments, looked around, took stock of where he was…and smiled. He knew what he would do: He kept the mirror covered and never looked into it. He made sure and thanked his mother, his father, the family that raised him, and white witchcraft‖.

22 Field of Nightmares

IF the Field of Dreams was built…and it turned *inside-out.*

The Kostners, Kevin, Thelma and their young boy, Billy, lived in rural Kansas and were avid baseball fans. Every spring, they'd get excited and watch all the baseball games TV offered. Then in the summer, they'd often have long road trips and enjoyed LA Dodgers games. But it was the local fields in the area of their small farm that they liked the best. Amateur baseball, amateur teams, where they saw new talent and potential greats before they entered the major leagues.

Billy, 12 years old, played in his school's Little League and was the most excited about baseball. Thelma was originally a football fan and followed the Kansas City Chiefs, but after she married her baseball-geek of a husband, she learned to love baseball over football.

Kevin was a baseball historian. If you named a year, he could tell you who won that year's World Series, scores and what teams made the playoffs. It was the early baseball of Ruth, Gehrig, Wagner, Cobb, Jones, 'Joltin' Joe' and other greats that Kevin was most interested in. He kept old scrapbooks his father made that contained newspaper clippings from the sports page of exciting moments in the game.

A shocking event or meeting happened at a nearby game the Kostner family attended between the Topeka Bulldogs and the Lawrenceville Wolverines…

In the bleachers, Kevin saw a face that he recognized. "I can't believe it, Thel, you know who I think that is?"

"No, who?"

The man left his wife and son and almost ran over to the other end of the small set of wooden bleachers next to third base. When he got close to the very old black man, Kevin yelled, "It's you!"

Immediately, the elderly baseball fan (who only wanted to enjoy a nice, quiet game) got down on the ground and backed away from Kevin. His eyes were large, his face had a frightening expression and he yelled, "No, I'm not!"

"Yeah, you are, c'mere," Kevin insisted and followed the guy.

"Get away from me! I'm not as young as I used to be."

They ran along the sidelines for a few seconds and then Kevin caught up with the man and grabbed him.

"Leave me alone!"

Mr. Kostner acted like an excited child. He shook

the old man a little and said with much enthusiasm: "But, you're James Earl Jones, the first Negro player in the major leagues!"

"No, I'm not!" The man acted very angry. "I only look like him, in fact, I think he's dead! Let me go, or I'll call the police!"

Kevin did not let go. He tilted his head and smiled even bigger. Their eyes met. "Ha, ha, haaa. Yes, you are. I never forget a face."

The black man changed from seriousness to a lighter mood. Jones smiled back at him and relaxed. There were tears in his eyes.

Kevin put his arm around the man's shoulders and turned him slightly. "C'mon. Some people I want you to meet. I'm Kevin."

By this time, curious Thelma and Billy were right behind him.

"There they are. Thelma, Billy, this is James Earl Jones…"

"Shoeless Jones!? The first black man in baseball?!" Billy yelled.

"No, no, child. There was a whole league before me with Page and Leon. I wasn't the best of 'em. They shudda went before me." Jones wiped his tears. "I must confess, Kevin. It's good to be recognized; that doesn't happen too much anymore 'cos of all my, my, uh, wrinkles, ha. Thank you."

"We're honored, sir. You went through a lot of shit for the game you love. We love it too…"

"Me, too," Billy said.

"My son's a pretty good slugger and shortstop."

"Are you now?" James Earl said and rubbed the top of his head.

"I got to see Shoeless Jones!" Billy exclaimed.

"Now, now, I should explain the nickname. Guys on the team thought it'd be funny to hide my shoes. They hid all the extra shoes from me. I had t' play. *One game* I played shoeless and t' name stuck with me fo'ever. I hit 3 homeruns that day and they didn't trick me so much after then."

Thelma insisted, "Please, sir. You have to come over our place for dinner. We'd love to hear your stories and I make the best peach pie in the state."

"Oh, she does," Kevin agreed.

Billy shook his head for *yes*.

James laughed and said, "Sure, I'll be there. Sounds divine."

A few days later, after the dinner, after the peach pie, and the stories from the golden days of baseball were over...

Kevin spoke to Jones and his family about the present-day and a few of the dreams he had...

"I want to show you something." Kevin got up, went to the front door and opened it. He was on the front porch and were soon joined by Thelma, Billy and James. "Look out there. All that land. Dreams have recently told me to do something that might upset my father, but then again, it really honors him."

"What the heck are you talking about, Kev?" Thelma asked her husband and was very confused. This was news to her.

"I know, Thel, I haven't discussed any of this with you..."

"This, what?" she asked.

"My plans, ah...look. We're doing very well. You

know I sold my computer company and had money before I inherited dad's farm. We don't need the farm and all the work that goes with it..."

"Really?" She was all-ears.

Kevin continued: "Yeah. James, what do you think? We clear out the cornfield and make a baseball field? Baseball, that's what my dreams are telling me..."

Thelma asked, "You're serious? Dreams told you?"

"I didn't know you wanted to do that, dad. Wow."

"Yeah. I'd mean we weren't farmers anymore, which might upset the old man; Billy's great grandfather was a farmer as well. We're from the land. I'd be giving that up, see? But he might be thrilled with the change into a ballfield in his backyard? Maybe?"

"I'm with you, Kevin," she said with a big smile. "He'd love it."

"And I would, too! My Little League team could play here instead of the dinky place we play. I'd be super!"

James said, "That sounds sweet, Kevin. But I sure won't be workin' in the fields for ya, boy. Ha, ha. Maybe, maybe I'll paint a few lines for yas, eh?"

"Yeah, ha, ha." Kevin added: "We'll have stands, bleachers over there and there. I'll build a wall for the homeruns. I should have thought of this before. It'll be great."

Thelma suggested, "Possibly you could convince the amateur league and have the Wolverines or the Juggernauts play here?"

"I was thinking of something way more magical and fantastic than that, Thel. My dreams showed me visions of Babe Ruth and Honus Wagner, and a young Shoeless Jones in their prime and playing baseball right here!

Wouldn't that be something? If we could sit here and all watch it play out in front of us?"

"But that's just a dream, Kev?"

"Yeah. Just a dream. I won't be runnin' 'round no bases. Look at me. I'm still alive. Ha!"

The next day, Kevin Kostner was outside among his tall corn stalks and pictured what he had seen in his dreams. He pointed and marked the diamond and length to the far wall. Suddenly, he heard:

"**IF you build it**…?"

"What?" Kevin looked up as if the voice came from the clouds. He stood still and listened again.

"**IF you build it…he will come**."

"Oh, my GOD!" Kevin turned and ran toward the ranch house. "Honey! Honey!"

Within two minutes, they both were in the cornfield close to the spot where Kevin heard the voice.

"I want you to listen. Listen close. Maybe it'll happen again?"

"Listen to what?"

"Ssssh."

Seconds later, the sky said: "**IF you build it…he will come**." It sounded like the Voice of God, and scared the willies out of Thelma. When she saw the thrilled look on the face of her husband, she realized, maybe the angels want them to build the ballfield? "Cool."

Weeks passed. The corn was cleared away. Ground was leveled. Real grass sections were purchased from Home Depot Gardening department and set in place. The wall was constructed and one set of bleachers was built. Sand was brought in and James Earl Jones painted the lines. The field was ready. Any team could play on it. But, will it be Kevin's Field of Dreams with baseball legends of the past?

Night after night, the Kostners sat on the wooden stands and wondered: What was going to happen? Will long-dead heroes of baseball actually appear? Shoeless Jones waited along with them on a couple nights. Then, one very late evening with a full Moon in a star-filled sky and James was there, it happened. Suddenly, there was light.

From between tall corn stalks, out walked: Honus Wagner, Lou Gehrig, Joe DiMaggio, Stan Musial, Casey Stengel, Lou Derocher, Babe Ruth, Mel Ott, Whitey Ford, Ty Cobb, Hank Greenburg, Vada Pinson and other greats from the Golden Age. They took the field.

The Kostners and James Jones were incredibly delighted – it was as if Kevin's dreams were now a reality. Or, were a reality to those who built the Magic Field. Amazing!

The players warmed up, tossed balls around and batted up. The game began. Suddenly, Kevin recognized a face on the sidelines and he couldn't believe it! *It was his father! When he was young and in great shape.* He wore a Yankee uniform and he was never a Yankee, but he always wanted to be. "Hey, d…you, you wanna catch?"

"I need to warm up. Sure thing."

Both tossed the baseball to one another with tears in their eyes. Kevin's best moments in life were catching ball with the old man. Now, he was a young man and the feelings were wonderful. Thelma and Billy and were in awe. What a magical moment. But it didn't last.

"Son. I have to tell you…" He threw the ball.

"What, dad?" Kevin wiped his tears and caught the ball.

"You should never have built the field…"

"What?! What d'ya mean? This would never've happened IF…"

"Watch," Stephen Kostner said to his son.

Whitey Ford struck out Ty Cobb and he ran at the pitcher to kill him! Everyone hated Cobb. HE was the one who'd come if the field was built so all the others could get their sweet vengeance on this terrible person. They beat him with bats. It was a ghastly scene. "No!"

23 League of Their Own

What IF the world was gender-reversed and boys and men were not the dominant gender? Women were the explorers, the scientists, the doctors and teachers. Girls were much stronger (willed). XX chromosome-ladies were the more intelligent gender and the more confident, forceful, aggressive gender...rather than passive boys and men with YY chromosomes, who really weren't that smart or tough. It was springtime and that means: baseball season.

During wartime, most ladies and heads of households who were of age, fought in the World War. So did members of professional baseball. The war devastated major league baseball with a great many girls that joined the marines, army, navy and air-force.

Connie Mack from New York, a well-known owner and coach (and gambler), did not want to let fans of baseball down, so she funded a very controversial move at the time. No pro baseball was played in 1942 and

1943. Baseball was the #1 sport in the country and America was saddened at the loss. But thanks to Mrs. Mack, a new league was created. Baseball fans could go to a few rural areas in the Midwest and *see the boys play!* Boys' League consisted of the best players from college. Only four teams: The Kansas City Broncos, the Topeka Buffalos, the Cleveland Corsairs and the Cincinnati Batsmen.

Boys were somewhat of a big joke in local newspapers, which ridiculed their level of play: "It's like seeing high school ball, nothing professional." "Riddled with mistakes, low-quality baseball." "Not like the women." "Why would anyone pay a dollar to see boys?"

On one of the fields in Ohio, Max (a Cleveland Corsair) asked his teammate, Bart, "You know who that is, coming?"

"That's our new coach; can you believe it? I think I recognize 'er. I forget who she played for."

"She sure doesn't look happy."

Bart repeated, "She sure doesn't look happy."

Her name was Harper Matlock, former baseball pro who played 16 years with the New Rochelle Rocketeers. Connie Mack gave her the assignment...*and she wanted to kill her!*

Later, she gave her first "pep-talk" to the Corsairs and it was obvious that she was drunk. Her speech was slurred and her foot slipped a few times. Harper Matlock didn't beat around the bush. She came out and flatly told them: "I don't care about you or the team. I don't care if we lose every game. I will stand there and make a show. I hate this fucking assignment! They have me by the cunt! I couldn't say no. So, ah, so, here the hell I am and don't ask me any questions."

Practice was every Tuesday and Thursday with the Corsair's first game in a week, against the Cincinnati Batsmen. Coach Matlock barely attended the practices, maybe one out of three. But one time, she came to a practice *sober.* Harper sat on the bleachers and the boys were in the field, and played. They were good. She was surprised. They were fast. She witnessed two home runs. A boy was thrown out at second base. The Corsairs were fucking great! They were as good as girls. This was a revelation to a lady who knew her baseball.

She said to herself: "If I have to be here, we may as well win."

From that day on, Coach Matlock was serious about her team and actively instructed them on every facet of baseball. The team picked up on the coach's new enthusiasm and played even harder, better.

When the game with the Batsmens was played, the final score was 17 – 2, the Corsairs! This gave Harper's team a lot of hope for the title because the Batsmen were considered the toughest competition.

The Cleveland Corsairs did it! They made it all the way to the Boys' League World Series. Against the Cincinnati Batsmen. They had played their rivals 3 times during the season and won all three games. But it almost seemed as if the Batsmen were padded with new players to even out the World Series.

The first two games were won by the Corsairs, 7-5 and 9-1. Then the Batsmen won the next three, 6-5, 14-10 and 3-0. The Corsairs fought back and won the next two Series games, 11-9 and 15-13. Sure enough, the Batsmen won the next game, 7-6, which led many to believe "the fix was in." The Corsairs never should have lost the game. The Series came down to a 9th game…

And…and…

The Corsairs lost 2-1 in what was called a "boring 9th game."

The newspapers were not kind to the Boys' League or the World Series, and they should have been. The Boys' League was a success. Connie Mack played it up as a "big success" in New York newspapers and few believed it. She was caught in baseball scandals and boxing fixes. Now, few people thought she was credible. The truth was: The Boys' League made a considerable profit. Larger numbers than expected attended the games and were "impressed with boy-baseball." Fans of baseball flocked to the four cities and happily paid their dollar. Newspapers criticized the "war-league," but that was not the opinion of thousands who attended in the two years it existed. They loved it. Although, most were sure that a real, professional baseball league for men could "never happen." The very next day…

THE WAR ENDED. The ladies returned home to their families. A shortened, pro, baseball season was played in 1944 when the conflict was known to terminate soon. America was delighted to see the women return to Major League Baseball.

Connie Mack was arrested.

Harper Matlock changed her tune after her experience with the team. She knew boys could play at the highest level of baseball. She was happy to have been with her Boys of Summer. She knew that she got to them, emotionally, with her last talk: "We may have lost a 9-

game World Series, guys. Please, don't be down. You did your very best; you are great players. Keep playing. But look around you. WAR'S OVER, be very happy and thankful for the things you have."

TS Caladan

24 Greatest Tennis Player of All Time

IF only the future of tennis was not taken over by PICKLEBALL!

When the Romulons (not the fictional Romulans from Star Trek) came to Earth in 2025, they discovered a very disturbing sight. *The lightspeed reports were true!* You see, Romulons, from the Sirius star system, are very big fans of our professional tennis. The aliens are humanoids that have 3 legs and 4 short arms. Romulons greatly admire the physical dexterity and graceful movements of human dance, ballet, many of our Olympic sports and especially tennis.

These superfans from Sirius go crazy when they view our tennis matches via television broadcasts into space! They know the pros of the past and they religiously monitor *present-day matches.* Romulons keep up with the game and listen to various tennis pundits who continuously broadcast transmissions through space. Problem is:

Romulons are always 8½ years behind Earth time. The bright Sirius sun that always flashes multi-colors is approximately 8.6 lightyears from Earth. Television signals take over 8 years to reach Sirius. Therefore, these superfans who worship tennis are embroiled in the race for who has won the most major tournaments. In other words, who is the 'Greatest Tennis Player of All Time'? Of course, this was the battle for major wins between Roger Federer, Rafa Nadal and Novak Djokovic. Romulons would have no knowledge of Next Gen players of today's game like Carlos Alcaraz and Jannik Sinner.

Understand that these aliens, these diehard purists who absolutely love the game of tennis…

Have just found out, in the year of 2025, *what Pickleball is!!!*

"No, no, no!" Captain Zon screamed from the cloaked ship a quarter mile above New Haven tennis facility's main court. "You mean, they're really doing it?"

Aris, the ship's First Officer, told his captain: "Yes, sir. The curse of Pickleball has grown and grown to such proportions that not only are park courts being changed to Pickleball courts, but large tennis stadiums are being converted to Pickleball stadiums. Very sorry, sir. We all feel the same as you feel, captain. Such a tragedy…"

"I know." Zon's 3 legs lifted him up from the command chair and he walked closer to the viewscreen. The Romulon captain just shook his head. "This is the scene directly below us. At first, I thought the stadium was simply in disarray and in need of repairs, but no. It's true. They are really changing the whole place into a Pickleball stadium! Augh!! How can this be happening to our beloved sport that we care about more than Earthlings do?! Do they *not see* the menace of Pickleball when it's right under their freaking noses and happening in about every country on this wretched planet? Pickleball, Pickleball professionals, rankings, tournaments, big money and stadiums?! Are you fucking kidding me?! What the hell's a pickle anyway, Aris?"

"Green food. I tasted it and almost *tangented;* it was disgusting!"

Captain Zon expressed, "Tennis is dying, or about dead…and those bastards don't even care?? They can't see the changes over time and what the world of tomorrow will look like? It'll be all professional Pickleball and professional tennis will hardly exist!"

"I know, sir. Saddest thing is: There is nothing we can do. Prime Directive and all. They have to fuck up on their own in a great many things and we have to just let them. Our 4 hands are tied."

The captain ordered: "Put on a recent high-level match, Aris. I want to see tennis played at the present time. We've seen nothing in the last 8+ years. I want to see how the game has changed in all that time. Have the

R.I. pick a final of a major tournament."

Ship's computer chose the last finals of the U.S. Open where Carlos Alcaraz defeated Jannik Sinner 6-4, 7-5, 1-6, 7-6. Captain Zon was amazed at the high quality of tennis excellence from these two young players. Tennis has indeed improved in the last 8 years with more speed and much more power. The lovely "touch," drop-shots excited the captain and the other Romulons who watched. "Oohs" and "aahs" were heard on the ship's bridge. The shots were wondrous, magical and fantastic in the eyes of those from Sirius.

Captain said, "It's hard to believe the game can be played like that and is very advanced from decades ago. Ugh. First Officer, I'm afraid to give the next command…"

"What sir?"

"Have the computer extrapolate 100 years in the future. What will tennis look like? Cover your eyes, crew, this won't be a pretty sight."

But when the crew saw what the R.I. projected, it was an *ultimate delight* that none of the aliens ever expected: a **LINELESS** smaller singles court in an oval-shape was the New Tennis and the *aliens loved it!!!* The captain expressed, "Ha, ha. I'll be damned. I guess Earth people got sick and tired of stupid Pickleball and perfected a better racket-sport?"

Romulons realized they still had a Big Question to answer. They created a Virtual Stadium, CGI. A Super Tournament of the very best players in tennis history. The Sirians made sure that every male tennis "legend" had the exact same:

*Training. *Coaching. *Facilities. *Starting age. *Age. *Practice. *Workout regimen. *Tour schedule, amount of play. *Experience. *Drugs. *Diet. *Physio. *Psycho-therapist. *Agents. *Rackets. *Rest time. *Entourage. *Off-court distractions. *Family...

The aliens made the competition for the Greatest of All Time as *even as they possibly could.* What would the Tournament come down to? Each player was in the same great shape as the others; their past and recent experiences were virtually identical. The players' natural physicality certainly came into play: height, length of arms and legs. But maybe the most important elements the Romulons tested were the Heart and Mind and Will and Drive to WIN! The players' mentality. The mental skills to strategize; to forget losses and wins; to size up an opponent during matches and *change* to suit various situations.

The final results were posted over Romulon Media channels as well as over "spaceway channels" onboard Starscreen tour buses:

Ken Rosewall, #12

David Nalbandian, #11

Ivan Lendl, #10

Lleyton Hewitt, #9
Pete Sampras, #8
Andre Agassi, #7
Rod Laver, #6

Roger Federer, #5   Rafa Nadal, #4   Novak Djokovic, #3

The superfans from the Sirius star system were very serious about their Earth tennis. They were really only concerned about who earned the top position and who made the top 12 as well as the set scores of the top 5 in the VR competition: Rafa beat Roger, 6-2, 7-6, 0-6, 7-6. Novak beat Rafa, 6-3, 6-4. 3-6, 1-6, 6-4.

Tennis fans around the flashy, bright, Sirius star were incredibly shocked that 3 pro players with the most major tournament victories did not make the top spot or even the 2nd Greatest Player of All Time. Nope. Bjorn Borg beat Novak Djokovic on clay in arguably the 2nd greatest tennis match of all time with the score: 6-7, 6-7, 7-6, 7-6, 7-6.

#2

#1

Almost unanimously among Romulons, the greatest match of all time was their FINALS on hard court, when Carlos Alcaraz defeated Borg: 7-6, 7-6, 6-7, 6-7, 7-6. A 12-point Tie-Break decided the 7-hour match. If the 5th set Tie-Break reached 11-11, then one point would be played to officially be crowned the Greatest of All Time. *The score hit 11-11 and Alcaraz won the Super Point after a 30-shot rally!*

Many pundits were very surprised that John McEnroe, Jimmy Conners, Boris Becker, Stefan Edberg and Jannik Sinner lost fairly early in the competition. Did they not have the heart and soul to win?

Carlos celebrated and highly enjoyed his supreme victory and, for a short time, thought he was the Greatest of All Time…

Until he realized he was only the greatest of this known universe and he'd have to play duplicates of himself from parallel worlds so that the Sirians would *really* know who was the Greatest. **"What?!!"**

25 Flog

RULES FOR FLOG

Long-range flogger for drives and long shots.	Short-range flogger for chip shots and putts.	Floghalls are 2-inch Wham-O superballs.

Flog (golf spelled backward) is played on a course much like traditional golf, only instead of a 'green,' there is a blue: a blue, roundish, curved carpet that simulates a real golf green. The 'hole' is called a 'void' and is a literal hole 1-foot in diameter & sits atop a round raised-up section on the blue, 3-inches above the carpet and 5-feet in diameter. Shots/putts must go up a blue incline before the flogball drops in the void. Players only need 2 clubs or rackets: a long one for drives and long-range shots, and a small racket for short shots and putts. The drive is like a serve in tennis and the high compression balls travel a great distance! You pick up the ball, stand on the spot it landed & serve again for the 2nd shot. When close to the blue and on the blue, shots should be hit with the smaller club and underhand. Pars are par 2, par 3 & par 4. The two rackets are kept in a quiver (like with arrows) and strapped under the shoulder.

IF golf was played differently and was a racket-sport, what would happen if the Legends of Flog gathered together one more time and performed for the television audience?

"Great to be with you all in Charleston. This is Gary McCord and Peter Allis is with me for the playoff round of the Legends' Tour. Well, this has been a wonderful event, great turnout, the weather has cooperated. Tell me your impressions of the tournament, Peter?"

"Well, I must say, they got us old folks out of the rest home, ha, for this…"

"Ha, ha, right. We haven't worked in a while, eh?"

Peter explained, "Like old times again, matched us up with the veteran floggers, I see, I see."

"I'm just happy to be here and see you again, my

friend."

"Aw. Me, as well. Impressions? Outside of the big 3 tie, I think the story has been how everyone, it seems, was so thrilled to see Lee (Trevino) make a run for the Legends' Cup…"

"That was the talk around the club. He sure was the people's choice, along with that energy and charisma that hasn't faded one bit."

Peter Allis commented: "Yes, yes. If you haven't heard or seen the last round, you might have missed it, but Trevino led the field until he reached the 18th blue and then…tragically, 6-putted."

Gary McCord said, "What a heartbreak that was for all of his fans, but then again, look what it left us with: a 3-way tie with the biggest names in Flog: Jack Nicklaus, Arnold Palmer and Gary Player. I mean, who could ask for more, Peter?"

"Brilliant. No one could have scripted anything better for flog fans. Here we go…"

Jack was up and pulled his flogger out on the 15th void tee. The large crowd around him hushed and remained quiet. There were only 4 voids readied for the playoff between the three. If they were tied after the 18th void, they would continue back on 15 until there was a winner.

Nicklaus' drives (as well as all the drives of the Legends) were nowhere near the distance he used to get on his shots from tee. Yet, they always received big applause from the interested gallery. There were many diehard fans of the Senior Tour that enjoyed the "old guys" even more than the young floggers.

On the first playoff void, Gary Player sunk a flogball from a sand trap and led Palmer and Nicklaus, 1 up.

The 16th and 17th voids were parred by the threesome, which meant Player was 1 up when they drove on the 18th tee.

Arnold had the best drive and had a clear view to the blue, away from large trees. Jack Nicklaus missed his drive, but luckily left it short of a fairway lake. Gary Player hit too hard of a drive and it went farther than he wanted it to go. An oak tree blocked his way. He could play to the side of the blue or slice the ball around the tree. *Why not go for it?* Gary used his flogger and created *spin*. The ball sliced left so much that the flogball went *out-of-bounds* – two stroke penalty. It meant that Player lost the lead and probably the tournament.

"That was a horrible break for Player," Allis said. "Maybe he should have worn his traditional black? The white clothes may have cost him the whole tournament. I can't see Arnie or Jack messing up. The Cup is between them now."

"I agree. Tough one for Gary. He has his army, as well."

Jack Nicklaus hit a fantastic 2nd shot. Arnold Palmer hit his 2nd shot safely on the blue. Arnold was farther away and would putt first.

"This is tense, my friend. Who'd have thought it would come down to two putts in a playoff?" McCord said with an excited tone.

"Surely all 3 deserve it, but we can only crown 1 of them king."

Arnold Palmer squinted in the sunlight and smiled for the crowd. With a small flogger in hand, he crouched down in his usual (but unusual) putting position. He was 40 feet away from the void. His arm went up as he gauged the slant in front of the raised section around the void. There was silence. A slight wind. He took a breath and struck the flogball. You heard people who screamed: "Get in!" "Get in the void!" IT WENT IN! ~ the ball took the curve and the incline perfectly, *and dropped in!* The crowd went crazy! They screamed.

Then, the crowd quieted.

Now, Jack's turn. His putt was 20 feet away. You could cut the tension with a knife. Everyone was sure he'd make it. A 20-foot putt was not difficult when a void is a full foot wide. Jack's putt looked good; it took the curve and incline well, *but it was off to the right by less than an inch and rolled down the other side of the raised circle.*

Arnie won the Legends' Cup!

It was said that the "sport of Flog won the day." The event promoters and fans enjoyed the tournament. It was a very big success.

26 The Story of Alfred E. Neuman

IF there really was a young, New York Jew named Alfred E. Neuman.

A new magazine called 'Mad Magazine' was in its very early production stages. Creators wanted a "face" for its monthly magazine and it wanted a *mad* face. Not a face that terrorized or the face of an insane killer. They wanted a silly, weird, strange, *funny* face to be their mascot.

Now enter: Alfie Neuman, a poor kid from the lower Bronx that was never successful in anything he ever attempted. Pitching pennies, he lost. Stick Ball, he lost,

Kick the Can, he lost. Playing tonk, he lost. Any type of investments, the boy always lost. If he wanted a bus, he had to wait. When he walked to the bus stop, he'd always just miss one. If he flipped a coin, it did not come up heads. A black cloud seemed to follow the poor, jinxed boy everywhere he went. *Why do I have such God-awful luck?* The kid was worried, very worried about his future and what to do in life. Parents always harped: "You'll never amount to anything and wind up in a poorhouse!" *How'd they know? Now they are dead and I don't know what the hell I'm doing.* He also worried how he'd get through life with the horrendous face God gave him. How could the boy have a good self-image when he was constantly harassed in high school? He was a depression that walked.

Alfie also lost his job at the "greasy spoon" and was about to be kicked out of a terrible apartment for nonpayment of back rent. Then:

The boy happened to walk by a big window of a Jewish deli on 14th Street. At the front table were Harry Akkerman and Sheldon Silverstein, the founders of Mad Magazine. When Shel saw Alfie walk by the window, he said: "Whoa." He ran out and confronted the boy. The kid was coaxed in and soon sat with them. They ordered the matzo balls.

"What's your name, kid?"

"Alfie, uh, ha." The boy's wide face laughed, showed his missing tooth and was overjoyed he'd get a matzo out of whatever these adults had in mind. The kid's face was covered in freckles, which made him very American and 'apple pie.' Just what they looked for.

"How would you like to be the face of our magazine? It's a funny magazine, all-cartoons! We have great artists that work for us, and…"

"What's it pay?" Alfie asked and smiled broader. He took a shot. It might pay off? You never know?

Harry said, "Well, well, we'll work on that, Alfie. It's a, a…"

The kid said, "I'm walkin' right now. I gotta know!" The boy stood up and presumed to leave.

"Hey, kid. Sit. Sit. You want money? Here's some money." Shel said and gave him $100. from his wallet.

Alfie was thrilled! He grabbed it, bit it, tossed it in his pocket.

"There's more where that came from. As soon as you sign a contract with us, we can advance you a stipend of, of, say…" Shel looked at his partner. "Oh, I'd say…five hundred bucks…?"

"Really? Five hundred dollars, for my face? Is this a joke?"

Harry replied, "No. Hey, kid. You're already hundred bucks up on the deal than you were minutes ago. Right, Alfie?"

"Hey, that's right. You know? I've been heckled all my damn lousy life 'cos of dis funny face of mine, boss…"

"I can imagine."

"You think I'm popular with girls? Huh."

"Look. You can get back at all the people who ever gave you a hard time, Alf. All you do is adhere to the conditions stipulated in the contract. By that, we mean show up when we want you to for photo shoots. Don't be late, intoxicated, drunk, or be on drugs…"

"I would never, sir."

"Good, good. That's about it. You agree that we can use your image for ads, promos, maybe back covers, who knows? Okay?"

"Okay," Alfie agreed. "What's the magazine called again?"

"Mad. Mad Magazine…"

"But I'm not angry at anyone. Honest."

"Ah. Out of the mouth of babes, eh?"

"No. We mean *crazy,* but actually kooky and funny, see kid?"

Alfie pointed at his big face. "So, you're sayin' I have a funny face, huh?"

Sheldon gave the boy a serious look, after he doused his cigar. "Look. We could use that funny face of yours and *pay you.* But the best thing is we will spread you all over town. Your face will be seen across the *country.* Mad Magazine will make you a star! Are you in?!"

"I'm IN!" They all shook hands, then ate the matza balls.

Shel and Harry were behind a glass wall in a rented photography studio. They overlooked a stage where black and white shots would soon be taken. Alfie was in front of the camera and cameraman, and on each side of the boy…there was a "dance hall girl" or local stripper. [Alfie's idea].

Harry commented, "Look at him. You Okayed this, Shel? Their boobs are almost hangin' out!"

"You don't think that'll sell? Is it MAD? *It's kinda mad;* I'll give that to him. Why would the babes be with someone that ugly, eh?"

"In a young person's magazine? With kids who read cartoons? I think the hookers will get us shutdown before we start," Harry replied.

"There's a point."

"Also, partner. Didn't Alfie give us the impression he doesn't drink or do drugs?"

"Yeah."

"Well, I received reports from our watchers and they sure smelled alcohol and noticed a change in his personality. We have a conduct-code. Drugs, right? *No one give him cocaine!* He'll think he's king around here and get a big head," Harry said seriously.

"Did you hear what you said? He'll get a big head?"

"Ha, haaaa! That's funny. He's... *My God, he's undressing her!* Yeah, now he's lookin' over 'ere."

"Let the kid go. He's having fun for the first time in his hard life. Big deal. We decide what pictures go in Mad. We won't use these, that's all," Sheldon told his partner.

"You're right on that point."

"Oh God, can't be touching 'er like that! I have to get in there!?"

A small board meeting of Mad staffers met in an office on Broadway and discussed the problem of Alfie Neuman.

"He has so many shitty suggestions; he thinks he has *power* because we use his photos and want him. They're garbage. But the one idea I do like of his is changing his name: Alfred E. Neuman. He wants a classy name since he's so high and mighty now. Funny, it works. I think we should go with Alfred E. in the magazine..."

"What's the E stand for? Ego? Ego-maniac? Eccentric, Eclectic?"

"Ellen. I kid you not. A family name, I'm sure."

"We'll keep it E. And if anyone asks, we'll say it's for: Einstein."

"Oh, that's good."

"I liked another of his hundred suggestions…"

"What was that?"

"What, me worry?"

"That's not a bad catch-phrase."

"He set up the shots of that ugly puss of his, in a bathtub of money, and surrounded with Vegas showgirls. Hey, ya attach 'What, me worry' with that photo and we got something, eh?"

"That works. But I'm afraid he's wacko now and very difficult to work with."

Then, Sheldon and Harry walked into the office room and hit the gang with the big news: "We just fired Alfie…"

"Really?" "Bout time." "Mad doesn't need his shit."

Shel said, "We're going with his image, which we own. He can't stop that. He'll always be the face of Mad. Artists will immortalize him on our pages. BUT. I'm afraid how he'll respond; will he Crack?"

Alfie cracked. All that fame and sudden notoriety! For him to lose everything?! It was far too much for his simple mind to take. The young man wound up in a NY sanitarium, stark, raving MAD!

27 Pets

IF the Zookeeper only knew the truth?

Tau Ceti is a bright, yellow sun in our stellar neighborhood. The planet with the highest population is TC-12. The Zookeeper was a famous personality on the planet for two reasons:

One: His expertise is *animals*. TC-12 is a virtual paradise-planet with 2,000,000 different types of creatures on a planet 25,000 miles in diameter (3 times the size of Earth). And two: the man was famous because he hosted a very popular educational show on the planet's prime Media. 'The Zookeeper' entertained the public and educated them on their lovely world. He believed in natural settings. No cages.

His organizations saw that people who wanted pets (most animals on TC-12 were docile and easily domesticated), got pets. Each person was screened for exactly the type of lifeform they desired and the Keeper's agencies made sure the pets matched the owners. The man marveled at how his pet movement caught on. The Zookeeper was beloved on his planet.

He was unaware that he was also a zoo specimen. The Builders, incorporeal beings of light, keep the TC-12 Zookeeper in their own type of ZOO without him knowing that fact. His every action is watched by crowds of aliens who file by remote viewers everyday – along with millions of zoo specimens in other locations in the galaxy.

28 Jose

IF only fate can be changed and death can be exchanged for life?

Jose was a good-looking dude. I don't know what his nationality was, maybe Filipino and Hawaiian? His real name was Joseph, but somehow that didn't fit him. Everyone called him "Jose." I remember from high school that many guys wanted to be Jose because of all the girls that were interested in him. Probably the most popular guy in school. One of the first kids who had long hair. He was considered a *rebel*. He also ran track, played baseball, played chess and was a good athlete. Jose even wrote a few songs and poems. He thought he was another Jim Morrison.

He started a keyboard band called 'The Electrons' with him, "Hose," as frontman. But the guys couldn't play their instruments; they were only in a band for the chicks, the beer, the weed and partying. They were allowed to play in our high school. But their 3 original songs were cut-off after one song when Jose excitedly yelled "Dammit!" The Electrons never played anywhere after that.

I remember his girlfriend: Dee Flint. Jose had all the girls he ever wanted to fuck until senior year. That's when he ignited with Flint. The blonde might not have been the most gorgeous girl in our class, but she was absolutely the "hottest." Jose and Dee were one of the "power-couples" in school who were often talked about more than other couples. Jose had everything going for him: popularity, a hot babe and even a new 'hot rod' his folks bought for him after graduation. Where did it all go wrong for the dude?

After high school was a completely different story. You could say, he got involved with the "wrong crowd." But who didn't at the time? We were the Class of '69! We even had our own song that some local 1-hit wonder band put out. Everyone played around, indulged and got hooked on drugs! It really depended on *which drugs* you played, indulged and got addicted to.

In our high school, cocaine and heroin did not exist. My hippie gang would have known about it if it was around. No. POT was the big drug at the time and the new experience most "hep" youths discovered. This was on the east coast, which was always behind the LA

California scene. Cocaine really did not hit the east coast until the early 1970s. Hard drugs were not as plentiful in suburban and country communities. It wasn't until college and after college, where there was more and more coke. [Pre-dating crack and crank].

But in certain areas and among small networks of drug-users, you could find the Hard Stuff, if you looked long enough, among the right groups of lowlifes. That's what happened to Jose…

It wasn't alcohol. It wasn't pot. Jose got hooked to cocaine and heroin! I've been around every drug, but heroin. Marijuana is not a "gateway" drug to harder drugs. My experience with coke, crank, speed, was really minimal compared to others of my time who went overboard. And it killed them. I did a lot of LSD and mescaline, which opened my brain up to Larger Things~.

Of all the people I have seen hard drugs ruin. Joe "Jose" Delach pisses me off and disturbs me the most. He and Dee had 3 children. Joe couldn't hold a job. He was found dead outside of Pittsburgh, on train tracks with a needle in his arm. Such a shame.

29 Homecoming

IF dreams came true?

It was November, 1972. I was 21 years old and just finished my 2-year stint in the army. I saw horrible things while I was in Vietnam, terrible things on both sides of the war. After what I'd seen some sergeants do, I wondered how different are we from animals? Sides, issues, the politics of Vietnam, did not matter. What mattered was staying alive in a wet, torrid hell-hole where there was no law and order, only madness. It was as if the war was only an exercise to bully and be bullied or enslave and be enslaved. No one questioned: What are we doing? We only obeyed insane commands from madmen and hoped to God we'd stay alive one more day.

All that's done, I thought as I found myself on my front porch. *I had so many close calls; shot on three different occasions. I only survived because I was near a medic each time, before they choppered me to a treatment center. How did I survive?*

I said, aloud, "It's like a dream. Can't believe I made it to my front porch in Bridgeville, 794 Bower Hill Road. Where I grew up and where my sisters and parents still live. Yeah, yeah, I think it was a good idea to not tell them exactly when I'd be home. They knew my duty was ending but, it'll be incredible to just walk in on them. *Surprise.*"

Suddenly, the front door of 794 Bower Hill Road opened…

"Aaah."

Kayanne and Rosemary briskly walked through the doorway and:

Through me! "What?!" It was as if I was a ghost, not there. "Oh, my God."

I heard my mother yell from inside the house: "I don't know if Kay should see that Godfather movie! All the sex?"

From the sidewalk, Rosemary shouted back: "I've already seen it, ma! There's not much sex; up against a wall a little bit, that's all."

"I don't know. Wait until I tell your father when he gets home."

Kayanne said to her sister, "I can't believe her."

"For God sake's mom, we're Italian! We should all see it. Bye!"

"Yeah, bye."

I heard my older sister's last words to her younger sister as they turned down the street: "Funny she didn't complain about all the *violence* in the movie. Ha."

I was cold, frozen. Still sitting. *You mean? You mean, it's true? That third time I was shot. I didn't make it? Huh!*

I noticed my M16 rifle, the weapon of choice, stood upright in the corner, next to the door. "Did they not see it? Is it a ghost-gun?" I picked it up. *Yep, feel's real. It's a ghost as well. I'm in limbo, I guess. I wanted to surprise them. Well, the big surprise is on me~.*

After a few minutes to get my head on straight and a few deep breaths, I realized: I had to do something. *I'll go see mom.* I stood up, turned toward the closed door and I took a step. Just what I thought would happen, happened. I walked through the door as if it wasn't there. *But I was the one not there? Or was I?*

"*MOM!!*" I screamed in her ear. Nothing. No reaction. I started boxing, really hitting her, but not hitting her. Every punch went through her as if she was made of air. "Wow." It was futile. I couldn't move anything in the room, but I could stand on the carpet. So, I kicked the carpet, again and again, as if to make a mark – something mother would be able to see. I could not do it. Nothing. Yet I stood upon it and felt it under my feet. I could move around in this dimension. *What is this place or reality I find myself in? Am I between the living and the dead? I wanted so much to hug her, but I couldn't! Mom was never for me going to fight in the war. It was dad who I was trying to please. Dad.*

She started doing the dishes in the kitchen.

I wanted to hug her so much, all of them. I thought it would be such a joyous and beautiful surprise. I took a few steps forward. I hugged her anyway and felt nothing. I felt a lot of emotions inside. But there was nothing physical, material, concrete. I cried. I had to leave, take a walk, something.

I left the ghost-M16 rifle in the corner. *Why not?* No one would see it, let alone use it. I took the same route my sisters took toward town and the movie theater. *Some homecoming. You mean I'm going to spend eternity in my combat uniform? Unbelievable.*

I passed a few neighbors and a few strangers on the way to town. Each one I prodded, poked, yelled at, and then cursed. It was to no avail. *Was I the ghost, or were they? To me, I seem very much alive.*

Minutes passed and I made it to the main part of Bridgeville, the front street where most of the stores were located. I noticed how certain buildings and signs have changed in two years.

Then…

Shock of shocks. I heard: "Doug! Doug Yurchey!"

I turned and it was…it was…*who was this?* "Oh, my God! Rick. Rick Tolmer! I don't believe it. Seeing you, seeing you, because, fuck, you're **DEAD**! Rick, you died 4 years ago. Hell, I was at your funeral. Lot of people were there; Mary Ann was there…"

"Yeah, yeah. Been a while since I've seen ya. You act surprised to see me. You know yer dead too?"

"Rick. I just found that out, ha, ha. Minutes ago, ha. It's just sinking in, man."

"Ah, let me guess. You were killed in a war?"

"Good guess, my friend, ha, ha."

"Ha, ha."

"So, so…what's it like?"

"Huh?"

I asked, "Well, we're not in heaven or hell; we're not at Rest; we're not at the Pearly Gates. Just what do we do to get into the light, you know, into heaven? You been stuck here all this time?"

Rick answered, "Believe it or not, I arrived here only a short time ago, but I've learned a few things…"

"Such as?"

"Oh, there is a marvelous place we call heaven that awaits us, yes, for some of us. But there are dark horrors and hells for others – it matters if you've amassed a bunch of merits or demerits in your lifetimes. I've talked to spirits, like us, and I found out: if you're still on the Earthly plane, and we are, then there's something we have to do to move on."

"What is it you have to do, Rick?"

"I don't know. Ha. We're all on different trips, man. You might find your way out soon, who knows? Maybe you should talk to Jimmy? He might be able to help you?"

"Jimmy?"

Rick replied, "Jimmy Mucha."

"I know Jimmy Mucha. Rick, you mean he's dead?"

"He died very recently by your clock, but he's been in town a long time. Time works differently in this reality. Jimmy is a dark spirit that casts spells and I've heard he can *touch* or *influence* the world of the living. If true, maybe he can help you move on? I don't know. That's his place there: just go into the large backroom of Sapersteins and you'll find him."

"Come with me. Maybe he'll help you?"

"No. I know I have to find my way on my own. And, anyway, Jimmy kinda gives me the creeps. But who knows what'll happen, eh? Best of luck on your journey,

Doug Yurchey." Rick shook my hand.

"And it was great seeing you again, Rick Tolmer. See ya, now."

Later, I did what Rick advised and walked through doors and walls and reached the back storeroom of the department store. I saw Jimmy. He sat on a velvet, violet couch. He wore a tight, black outfit. He appeared to be a mystic that was in the middle of conjuring a powerful spell…and that was exactly what he was doing.

I wasn't going to wait. Frankly, I never liked the kid. I went up to him and interrupted his whole magic ritual…

"Jimmy Mucha," I said close to his face, which opened his eyes.

The kid in my home room and 1st period Art class years ago SCREAMED AT ME! *This is perfect!* As fate would have it! Hey, Doug! Look over here, through this window. Tell me what you see?"

Jimmy appeared wild-eyed, insane. My impression was he was the king of the ghosts, the big boss man. *Dark Spirit,* Rick said.

I wasn't sure exactly what Jimmy meant until I glanced through the window and saw two people who talked in the street.

Mucha said, "I tested my powers on the physical world and caused a car crash, just a moment ago, that killed your father. Steve's dead, and then you come walking in. Uh, HA! That is precious!"

I was so angry, I wanted to kill him, if he wasn't already dead! "Why would you do that, Jim?! What do you have against my father?"

"You don't remember, Dougie? You don't remember the big game? When your father, the umpire, struck me out?! My parents were there watching closely and those 3 pitches were balls, not strikes! Bases were loaded! It was my chance to be the hero. Fuck!!"

"Yeah, Jim. He struck me out too. *Your hocus pocus just killed my father in a crash?* This isn't a dream, it's a nightmare!"

"Ha. I'm going to tell you what I'm going to do next, soldier boy, because you are helpless to do anything about it, eh? There are a few dozen souls stuck here in Bridgeville limbo-land, this *bridge* between heaven and hell. They're my slaves. They must obey me and they do. Now your dad will obey me and I'm not done toying with him, ha. Wait till you see what's coming next, pal!"

"Why?! What the fuck?!" I screamed. *Did I lose my mind?* Then the thought came and I went with it: I attacked the boss ghost! *Why didn't others fight him? I'm not going to be mesmerized by Jimmy.* I choked him! He laughed at me.

Jimmy quickly opened a drawer and grabbed a knife. He swung it and it cut me. *Wait a minute, I'm a ghost that bled and felt pain?*

He explained, "The knife was transferred from the other side. It's a ghost-knife and you and the others will feel its *sting!* It will take time, but many deadly items will change over to this side. I will inflict such pain on all you ghosts...*that you'll wish you were dead!!"*

This was too much. My only thought was to run, run out of the storeroom and onto the street. I ran out, right passed Rick and my dead father. There was no time to lose. If Jimmy, however the fuck he got his powers, was not stopped soon, who knows what demons will materialize in Ghost World?

I had a plan. *Would it work? Would destroying the*

devil be that easy? I ran home. I ran to 794 Bower Hill Road as fast as my legs carried me.

Later, I returned to Jimmy's warehouse lair. He again sat on the velvet couch in the middle of a big, mystical spell. And <u>my father stood there motionless, like a zombie,</u> inside a painted circle on the floor. I had to stop Jimmy from doing whatever he was doing…

So, point blank, I aimed and ***fired*** *my Ghost-Gun, the M16,* that apparently materialized with me on my front porch when I first got here! If the knife hurt ghosts, I figured the rifle would do damage.

Jimmy Mucha bled ghost-blood on the floor, and because of his destruction: Everything that he influenced, moved and transferred over, was no more. All was back in its place before Jimmy's arrival…

But one more CHANGE occurred: Doug Yurchey never fought in the Vietnam War. He wasn't in the army in 1971-1972; he was in college. Another timeline took the place of the old one. In the new reality (dream), he was a long-haired hippy. He spoke out and marched against the Vietnam War. But today…

Steve *pounded* on the door of his son's off-campus room in the little town of Edinboro, PA. "Hey, Dougie! Open up, damn you!"

Doug opened the door.

His father and cousin, Reed, rushed into the room. His father was pissed and paced from one side to the other. He yelled, "Alright! Where's your pills?!"

"What?!"

"I got a call from your tennis coach and just traveled 130 miles so you can explain it to me, boy! You were seen in Erie on pills! Now, where are they?!"

Reed shook his head and didn't know what to say. (I guess dad needed someone to sound off to on the way up Route 79).

[I was innocent and did not trip that weekend in Erie. It was another weekend I tripped. *I just now woke from a dream that came true?* I remembered the other timeline where I was a dead soldier and dad was also dead. In this reality, it was only a dream, ha, and I was a long-haired hippy. I was very, very happy to hear him scream at me].

30 The Wrong Door

IF only you chose another door.

There was an unusual Carnival at Coney Island. When I got there, *why did I think of that weird, old movie, 'Carnival of Souls'?* Funny, I had just seen it on cable and I couldn't shake the black and white images out of my head. In the movie, a blonde girl wanders into what appears as an abandoned carnival, much like this one I saw from a distance. She was drawn to it, then saw these weird ghosts dancing and *she ran the hell out of there! Maybe I should do the same? I feel like leaving; I feel like running out of the menagerie, whatever this carnival really is on Coney Island? But…I just can't.*

I heard a siren. There were tents and more tents lined up on both sides of the boardwalk in the middle of the day. People milled about, went in various tents of their choice and also played on the beach and in the ocean. I smelled hotdogs. I was curious and walked up to one of the tents. Strange. There was a door on each tent, not a real door, a painted door of cloth. I pushed through the cloth door and I found an odd man and two ladies inside. They wore bizarre headgear [his hat had horns] and they held a few items in their hands: a wine glass, a rose and a Devil Tarot card. Very curious. I smiled and wondered what this exhibit was about.

The man said, "Have you ever heard of the 3-door test where you must choose between a lady and all the riches in the world, or another door with a tiger that will kill you, or a third door of mystery?"

"Ah, ah, yeah. I think I've heard of that…"

"Well. This is nothing like that."

The blonde and redhead smiled, giggled a bit…then got serious.

"Okay, it's a little like that, but different."

"Go on. I'm listening," I was very skeptical of this joker. Was he a magician? I was watching him very carefully. I wanted to figure out how the trick was done, whatever the trick will be?

"George, you must choose one door, only one door, and that door will be your fate…"

"Hey, you know my name!" I was surprised. *Was this guy legit?*

He smiled. "I want you to walk outside; go back the way you came. And then come back and tell me what you see. Okay, George?"

"I can do that." I left through the cloth entrance and, and, and…

IT WAS NIGHT? It wasn't night! It was late afternoon, sunshine, people playing in the ocean…now, it was pitch black, no one in sight? Only thousands and thousands of the same kind of tent: two rows on each side of the boardwalk. Tents seemed to have stretched for miles! *What is this? Nice trick!* And each tent had a door on it. *What?*

I went back in. There they were. I told them just what I had seen. I was frantic. Did this joker control my mind? Direct what I'm seeing? Who is he? The devil? He held the Devil Card.

"Haven't you figured it out yet, friend?"

"No. Tell me."

"What happened to the girl in the movie?"

"What movie?" I asked.

"The one that's in your head? The carnival of souls? You really don't know?"

The girls laughed at me.

"Ah, ah. Oh, yeah." I remembered. Before, I didn't want to remember. But now I remember. "She died. She died in the beginning and was dead the whole time! Wait! *I'm dead?*"

"This isn't a dream, George. Ha, ha."

I got a chill down my spine when I realized he was the devil. I freaked out. "And you're the devil?"

He smiled so large that I saw his fangs. "Aaaaaah…could be?"

"And I'm in hell? You know, I wasn't that bad of a guy in life. In fact, I was a righteous dude. I think I helped a lot of people, *devil!*"

"That doesn't matter, Georgie."

"What matters?" I asked. I thought it was an important question.

"What door you choose. You can get out of this, have the girl and everything, in a sense. Here's what you do: Go outside again and, you know, just for you, my friend? I will give you TWO choices! You get 2 chances to pick the right door. Hey, I ain't a bad guy…"

The girls really laughed at that one.

"Look, Beelzebub. I still don't get it. I'm dead…?"

"Ah, ba, ba, ba, you might not be," the devil told me. "Not if you pick the rose. That's the right choice. One of those doors outside in the carny is your get-out-of-death card and also your great fortune card, but you must make the right choice. A super tremendous future could await you behind the right door. I'm serious; *back to the world of the living.* And a sweet, sweet life of happiness that goes with the right door. What will the cup be filled with? Nothing, fantastic-tasting wine…or poison? Choice is yours, George. You must decide or stay here in limbo forever? I would go out and make the choices if I were you."

"You know, buddy? I was never the luckiest guy. But I'll give it a shot." I went outside and when I looked across the way, I liked my odds better – there were only three tents. Two choices out of three to pick the rose? I didn't even think about it and simply reacted with my gut feeling. I chose one and walked into the cloth door. There was nothing inside. I realized this tent was the empty cup. Oh, my God. What was left was the 'wine' or the 'poison.' I came out of the tent and…*this was it!* Was it going to be the tiger or the lady? Everything or nothing, life or death? I had to choose one. "Eenie, meenie, minee, moe." *This must be the right door.* I walked through it…

31 Saved

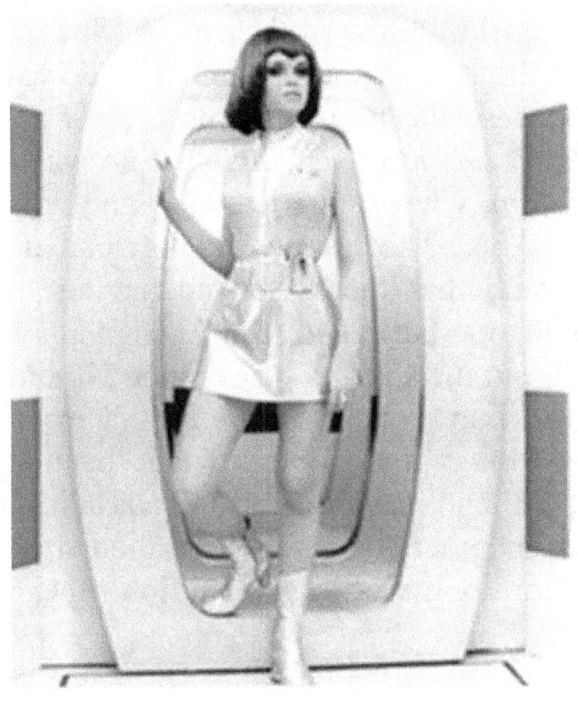

IF only the 'Heaven's Door' cult members were a bit wiser and questioned the messages they received over their computer screens?

The Heaven's Door "cult" had been in existence since 1999 when 'Trip' and 'Founder,' their "high priests," claimed to have received videos and audio tracks from space. There was no way of confirming or denying the videos came from space. For 20 years, Founder and Trip have promoted the videos and gained a modest following. The HD group consisted of more than 300 members at last count. The overall message of the collective was one of future peace, love, abundance and riches – not for Earthlings in general, but for those who followed them and became a member of Heaven's Door. The public was certain HD was a scam for money. The group heard from a Space Woman called Glenda and saw the beautiful girl in a few of the videos. She resembled a character on the British show: UFO. The ET videos were not clear because the transmissions came from millions of miles away. *Glenda was coming!* She was coming to Earth in a large, white, spherical ship and would SAVE all who joined her! The cult pushed how bad and polluted the planet was, that there was no saving it. Nothing anyone could do, but LEAVE IT. Glenda's ship truly came to Earth in the shadow of a comet. No one believed anything the group broadcast…*until every member of HD disappeared one day!* They were beamed aboard Glenda's ship and saved. But Glenda did not mean "saved" like members believed. The alien *saved* them in her computer, along with a few million other programs. Preserved.

32 The Death Chair

IF only I didn't see the 'Frasier' where he and his father fought. It was the one where Martin finally got on Frasier's high-class nerves. Everything his "dad" did annoyed him: how loud he chewed potato chips, how his chair squeaked, etc. Martin attempted to appease Frasier when he oiled the chair. He turned the chair over and a can of black oil accidently spilled on Frasier's brand-new carpet! A very expensive European carpet, the color 'buff.' Frasier hit the roof! His carpet was ruined. He believed it was a subconscious act that was basically *intentional*. Days later, Frasier and Nils moved furniture out of the way for a new rug to be laid. His father's precious, ragged, old chair was placed on the balcony ledge. The Sun's rays through a telescope ignited the chair on fire. When Nils and Frasier saw the fire, they rushed to it and accidently pushed the chair over the balcony! *It nearly hit Martin and Daphne.* Of course, the episode ended warmly. Frasier specially ordered a duplicate made and the ratty, old chair became the most expensive piece of his furniture collection.

"I don't believe it," I said out loud. Talking to the 4 walls was a habit I picked up from my father. *My father who had just died.* I heard him talk to himself plenty of times when he didn't know I was listening. How did I never notice the striking similarity between the famous chair on the show, and my father's living room chair? No, he never saw cool, funny shows like Cheers, Frasier or MASH. He watched the news, mainly, and got really uptight about it…but, the CHAIR! It was the same chair, except that dad's was a little greener. It was the chair I found him **DEAD** in! ☠ Actually, he was working on it when I walked in and found him like that, next to it. The chair was turned over. His tools were spread all around the carpet. Maybe it was a squeak he tried to fix? He collapsed right there…*dead.* He was a working man; worked all of his life. He worked to the very end.

That damn Frasier episode about the feud between father and son, triggered the Chair realization, how similar it was to our living room chair. Especially when I saw it turned over and Martin worked on it. That's how I found the chair when I found dad dead. And that chair was as important to Steve as it was to Martin. Father wasn't an affectionate guy. I was. I remember I kissed his cheek, his cold cheek. That's not all that happened because of the show…

Deep, emotional thoughts often invade dreams and they did that night. I dreamed I made a milkshake for my father and a hit of LSD came out of my shirt pocket because there was a hole on the bottom. And I didn't notice the hole or the missing tab of acid until later…

Later, I saw my dad who acted funny. By that I mean *emotional.* I never saw him emotional before. Maybe a tear at a funeral or when he watched a movie, but that was rare. In the dream, he told me how much he loved me. *He cried in my arms!* ["What?!"]. I know this wasn't real because my father never once told me he loved me. Not in real life. But, in my vision, he blubbered like Niagara Falls! He said how he should have treated mother better, much better. Rose had been deceased for the last 5 years. Steve confessed he should have spent more money on her, bought her better clothes, taken her out more often and traveled with her, once I was no longer a child. Amazing, that I heard these words come out of his mouth or heart. He told me he should have treated me better, been more supportive, more positive, rather than the negative-influence he was. He was very sorry, sorry for a great many things. It was wonderful to cry in his arms.

I take it back. I'm happy. I'm happy I saw that Frasier show. I'm glad I had the chair realization and it created this sweet moment between Steve and I in a dream that never would have happened in the real world. My tears were happy tears of joy. Thank you.

33 Where are you going?

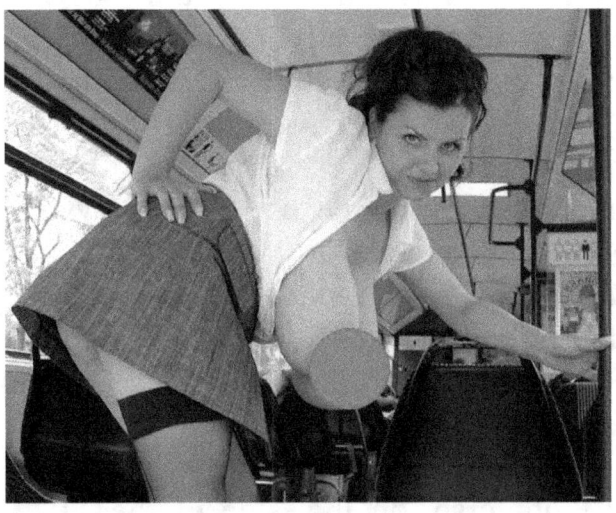

IF only good things lasted forever, as in a literal eternity, but they don't.

"Where are you going? Where are you all going?! Melba! What are you doing to me?!"

"I'm rounding up the girls and we're all, and I mean *all,* taking the bus and heading out of your sick neighborhood, Mister Rodgers! We've had it!"

"What?!! You kidding me? What's not to love in my 'playground of the mind' where you can take your shoes off and everything's perfect and beautiful and sexy and can last however long we, we…"

"I've talked to the girls and they're *fed up with this place!* You said we could use the Tele-Pyramid and create and live in a world of our own design, one we build…and see what happened!"

"Well, Y'all did that; I gave you the same ability I

have to make thoughts real and when you went in the TP to do that...*you didn't come out again!* I mean, what the fuck? I thought you'd come back and...*visit,* thank me and we could rekindle old times again 'cos we can stop time and space and literally *have all the time in the world!* Bouncey, bouncey, but NO! Hardly any of you returned, came back. There's gratitude for ya! Now, now, yer group-leaving?"

"Can you really blame us? Look how long you've had it your way, Rodgers!"

"But, Melba! No one put a gun to the ladies' heads. You had free choice, free will! You could all enjoy a wild/amazing paradise in a perfect, fucking body FOREVER!"

"Dude, dude! Are you mental?! With *you* as the only guy in the universe, on this side of the TP? The girls constructed their own lives inside it with their true love or the men they knew, or any boys they ever wanted to fuck. You know, *what you did?!* They wanted no part of you once they had power and control in their hands."

"I wasn't cruel. I was kind, good to y'all. We had a lot of *fun,* a lot of pleasure...remember? What? I couldn't make a friend? I didn't want ALL of you girls. I wanted a few solid, meaningful relationships like a family. I wanted to be loved. But yer all leaving me now (sob)?"

"You can make other girls, right?"

"But I'll lose hundreds of the ones I had! Beautiful flowers that will never wilt; beautiful, perfect snowflakes that will never fade away. Sure, I can make more. But I lost the relationships I thought I had! Fuck. I can't believe all of you are leaving me."

"Sorry. It was fun with you while it lasted. But we're moving on. They agreed to meet me here, and when I drive the entire/elongated bus through the Tele-Pyramid, we'll be *free,* on our own and never have to see this place again. Good-bye!"

"Oh, God. Here they come now. They're really going with you? Oh, no! Danni Ash, not you. Chloe Vevrier, Lorna Morgan, Christy Canyons, Aunt Peg! Giselle Bundchen, Latitia Casta, NO! This is not happening! Malvina, Donna Michelle, Christa Speck, damn, Dorothy Stratton, not you, too! *I thought you loved me!* Oh, boy. There goes Roberta Pedon, no, no, no! I thought we had something, babe! I made you my fantasy sister! What the hell's wrong with a little incest in 'the playground of the mind'? Fuck me!! Liv! They're all leaving!? Man, did I waste my time and energy on y'all. This is such crapola. Shit."

"Bye, Mister Rodgers." "Bye." "Write." "Ba-bye." "Ba-bye."

The bus pulled out and I coughed at the fumes and dust it created. "My bus would have been perfect. No fumes. Geez. They're all gone? Hey, what's that? Who's that? *Oh, my freaking God.* One of them stayed. I wonder which one of them it is? Oh, honey. It's…"

*Author's comments on the 33 Stories:

1. Peep and the Tree of Evil came out of looking at the 'Pexels' site and seeing if there were interesting fantasy photos I could use. The two I chose looked great and a weird story originally called "Minion," became very different than 1st planned. Like 99% of my short stories, I start with either a cool title, or picture, or both. I sit down to write and know the stories will work; they will be good…but I have no clue of the endings. The stories write themselves as I write. Like jumping off a cliff and building a parachute on the way down. It never fails. Each time, I'm pleased with how everything came together in the end. The final image was a dude that pulled himself from a tree branch and that photo determined how the story ended.

2. The Great Insect Rebellion was a story I instantly started to write as soon as I saw a free pic I could use of bugs who stood upright. I wrote until they reached the cabin, then went on and wrote other stories. I knew I'd get back to it and figure out the plot. I was happy in the end. Originally, I included spiders, then used them to stop the war.

3. The Aurora is God was a story I started, then left it for about a *week*. The plan was to come back and include a # of Mandela Effects. Voyage up Cook's Strait I saw on YT, *and it really creeped me out.*

4. Pandragon of Prague came out of my desire to write a story about *dragons.* I never had them as a main character before. First, I created a 'Pandragon,' which sounds like the magician: Pendragon. Since "pan" was in its name, then it had to include a panorama of all the dragon spirits before him. He wasn't a terrorist dragon; he hardly damaged the town. There was something else that bugged him, and I didn't know what that was until I got to the end. I guess I make the endings fit and they always seem to – but I sure don't know where I'm going when I begin. Is the idea of dragons driving spaceships new?

5. Noseferatu was a joke I immediately came up with while I tried to watch the new Nosferatu movie on a free movie channel. I can barely stomach any movie done today. But I was quick with a NOSE feratu joke and that's all it took. I found a photo of Max Schreck from the silent film, enlarged his nose and *it cracked me up to the max!* I thought it was hilarious. Then, I left the story and wrote other stories. Again, I knew I'd be back and compose something funny, and you also had to toss in something very gruesome. Max was always going to be a real vampire, although I considered other possibilities. Well-aware readers know the concept of a vampire-actor who played a real vampire was never done better than Willem DeFoe's portrayal in *Shadow of the Vampire.* It was a brilliant idea to redo the filming of 'Nosferatu' with Max Schreck as an honest-to-goodness, blood-sucking vampire – so *what you saw in the silent film appeared morbidly real and chilling.* The film crew wound up dead in that version also. But I really didn't know the end of my story until I got to the last scene: I mean, the whole JOKE. I hardly made a connection to the nose throughout the story, and had to for a big-ending punchline that connected with NOSE. But what could it be? Then like a lightning bolt, *there it was!* Sister Cocaine! They dabbled in coke and opium at the time. I figured a rich/royal London film crew might have cocaine for the Wrap Party!

6. The Family Curse, I confess, was previously written and in one of my two early short-story books. I wanted to redo it and it certainly fit with the themes of: vampires, Transylvania, werewolves and dragons.

Maybe the ending was an obvious twist: the *werewolf family changed into humans,* Okay. But you probably didn't figure out that pissed off Flem would eat the family and turn into a were-person herself, eh?

7. Jason and the Harpies was a nod to *Jason and the Argonauts*. I remembered when mortal thieves like Jason's men touched the Fleece, it faded. I wrote a scenario that the crew thought it was worthless and their quest was in vain, so: *mutiny!* The harpies I loved, and the food-torture they unleashed on whatever the heck his name was. Poor man. I enjoyed the harpies' dialog. I wanted to do the 3-Question-thing and, I swear, it took only minutes to imagine the questions and realize the ending. Of course, Jason would turn out to be a hero. *Want a taco?*

8. Robin Hoodlum was actually an easy one to write, because Robin's story is so ingrained in me. I grew up on

the old English series with Richard Greene as Robin
Hood; I saw it on TV every morning before I left for
school. Me and a few kids played out Robin's story when
we made Cook School Woods our Sherwood Forest.
Believe it or not, Jimmy Mucha was Robin – I was Will
Scarlett - and Maid Marion was played by Georganne
Sinclair, Jimmy's girlfriend. Didn't everyone do this? So.
When I decided to do a story with the familiar characters,
the plot was hammered out in minutes. It's a clever plot
and I knew all would mesh together nicely in the end.
But I didn't have a good title. Although I knew if I sat
down and put my mind to it, I'd find it. After a lot of
thoughts were thought on the problem, it was a *Lightning
Flash*…the perfect title.

**9. IF Clark Kent was Batman and Bruce Wayne was
Superman**, could be my best one! Could be my funniest
one. I know it was the hardest story to write~. Why?
Because the Superman and Batman stories, themes,
colors, abilities, situations, adjacent characters, are so
deep in our psyches that it was very difficult to keep
track: who was who? I love the crossover jokes like:
Batman making the point that bats fly, no? Batman
wanted to ride in the cool Supermobile. And Superman
wanted a Boy Wonder to ride shotgun with him.
Superman asks Batman what went on, because he *didn't*
have super-sight. I enjoyed the direction of the story;
how concise plot points were and how quickly I reached
the joke. What could be to Batman what kryptonite is to
Superman? Again, it was instantaneous! Wolfsbane! The
bane of the bat! Clark (Batman) was so dumb! And
Bruce (Superman) was so super-smart! I hope readers
enjoy the story as much as I do. You just knew they

would wind up as Super-Friends.

10. What Ever Happened to Brainiac 5? Had to be the follow-up story. What happened to the Kryptonian city of Kandor? I thought the old DC memory could be retooled. B-5 fit right in with the A.I. of today and maybe a war with machines? Who remembers the exact story? I created a conduit-vortex Brainiac had that Superman used to fetch the Bottled City from Krypton and preserve it in his Fortress. I was also happy to toss in the red machine with the black button and the white button, which zapped you in and out of the Phantom Zone.

11. 7 Faces of Doctor No. The next two short stories were rattled off quickly. When the funny title hit me, I knew I had to write it. But who knew where the story will lead or where I'll go with it? News to me.

12. Plan 1 – 8 from Outer Space was also an old story in concept and I tried to find it, and I couldn't. Just as well. In no more than 10 minutes, I had my 8 plans that I think were funny and made a point.

13. Forbidden Moon was an obvious take on *Forbidden Planet*, as if Mars once had many-eyed/many-legged inhabitants. And, suddenly, Deimos (moon) came along and appeared in orbit. Two missions were sent to investigate (like the movie). It's found the moon is **alive**, and in a Hide-n-Seek game with Phobos. Both become permanent moons.

14. The Day Mars Stood Still is almost my favorite. I couldn't get enough of the original movie with Michael Rennie as Klaatu, who warned governments of Earth that atomics on rockets will not be tolerated. Well, I used my years of studying Mars and concepts I've placed in articles and other stories…and adapted the movie's main scenes to my Martian story. The new, red, rebel military Stood Still for a day, and contemplated Lattu's ultimatum. Safety of the 5th planet was at stake. But sadly, the rebel's decision automatically activated the deadly Robot and *Mars was destroyed!* But Lattu saved the family that helped him. Coffee was the lady's name because the actress was later known for coffee commercials. Doctor Dinn was the Einstein-character (Sam Jaffe) in the movie and the actor played Gunga Din.

15. Zorro, Lost in Space was maybe the most fun story to write in this collection, besides Superman/Batman. I combined two roles Guy Williams played from many years ago. Easily done with genius Will Robinson (Billy Mumy) and a transporter he rigged. How else could the two characters exchange places? And Maureen loved the "stash."

16. Sungate, a parallel to the Stargate series, was another quickie that I thought was very funny. The clue was 'Jack Tripper,' right from the beginning. I knew the SG series well. How to end it? The little alien.

17. RATAVA, reverse of AVATAR. What would happen if Pandora, with the blue creatures, was so inundated by human visitors that the natives loved them and wanted to be like us, we creatures of a modern technology? Well, best laid plans…*can blow up in your face!* Because the blue natives got in chambers and were rudely awakened on Earth.

18. A Boy and his Cat*, my version of the movie with

Don Johnson and a dog ['Boy and his Dog']. It came on TV, like many of these stories. A movie is in front of my eyes and I think: *I can put a weird twist to it.* I took notes during the movie and left a lot out of the story. But it was longer, more detailed than I originally imagined. Why did Billy Jean look like Melanie Griffin? Because Melanie Griffin was married to Don Johnson in real life. I figured out how to use my 1st love in cats: Eno's (*see 'Pets') name and photos I took of my 2nd love in cats: Sheno. The way down into the movie's underworld was a dark, metallic structure. I made mine a tree with striations, to fit Sheno's photo from the backyard. *I'm DH Jetson.*

19. The Pittsburgh Experiment was also a fun story to write because I come from Pittsburgh and remember the area well. I've used East McKeesport before. I matched the story to the picture I found. I also used my knowledge of the Philadelphia Experiment and made its parallel in Pittsburgh. Nikola Tesla was involved in the original Experiment and in my fictional one. The great inventor was connected to Pittsburgh through George Westinghouse, one of his backers. What might seem like fantasy, *is not fantasy* – but real-world stuff – if you study details of the Philadelphia Experiment: The aliens, the Lizards, the conduits or vortexes between space and time, the disappearances of the 'Montauk Boys' ['McKeesport Boys'] are REAL. Even that a monster Beast known as "Junior" was materialized out of Duncan Cameron's special mind…is real, and reflected in my story.

20. Day of the Dead Living. It was difficult just to twist the title and use one that hasn't been used before. *Night of the Living Dead* was a classic George Romero film. Pittsburgh people recognized Chilly Billy Cardille, host of 'Chiller Theater,' a local TV show with twin chiller movies every Saturday night. So, I made him Arsenio Hall. Remember, this was a black world where all the white people were dead and it was white people who came back to life and crawled out of their graves? What am I saying? What's my point? Well, the tied-up, white zombie made a few good points and he was shot for talking.

21. The Mirror of Dorian White was actually the last story written, then inserted along with the other movie spoofs. You have to know The Picture or Portrait [it's a Mandela] of Dorian Gray to understand fully. *The painting got old and creepy while the man stayed young and pretty for many years. In the end, they reversed positions, the man died and turned hideously ugly.* Like a lightning bolt, I created a Mr. White and a Mr. Black, who'd meet like 'Strangers on a Train.' They were estranged twin brothers, but opposite – you could say "mirror twins." Soon, it was clear what the plot would be. But how could the dead brother, Mr. White, come back? Through the mirror, of course.

22. Field of Nightmares was a sheer joy to write. Rekindled a lost love for baseball in me. Especially when I caught ball with my dad, my greatest and happiest memories. Once again, I wasn't sure of the ending. I sort of forgot about the twist title and had to conclude in a nightmare. (I used real names of Kostner and James Earl Jones). Here's what's very strange: This is a Mandela

Effect. Everyone who has seen the movie 'Field of Dreams' should remember that the Voice in the sky said: **"If you build it, *they* will come."** Right? What happened in the end? They, all the local people, came to the magic ballfield. But. *No, no, all that's changed* because if you see any copy of 'Field of Dreams,' the Voice says something different. The Voice now says: **"If you build it, <u>he</u> will come."** God's truth. See the movie and you'll see I'm right. Versions of "they" will come, no longer exist in this universe, yet most people remember THEY – "they," not "he." That's gone along with Jiffy Peanut Butter, Sherman-Williams Paint and Ed McMahon as a spokesman for Publisher's Clearing House. So much we remember is totally gone now and not coming back. I used "he" in my story to connect to a Ty Cobb-ending (who really was hated), but I know damn well the Voice said: "they." And so do you.

23. League of Their Own is just a precious little story of mine. I love it. To appreciate it, you have to be familiar with the original movie with Rosie O'Donnell, Geena Davis, Madonna and Tom Hanks as a cantankerous ex-player now assigned to coach a *team of girls* during wartime. It's a Woman's Universe in my version and genders are switched. Women fought in the World War, not men. Women played major league baseball, not men. We follow a complete reversal with a cantankerous lady coach assigned to coach a Boy's League team! The same ending happened in my story where the coach has a change of heart and respects the play of the other gender. What am I saying? I'm saying: In this new climate of strong Warrior Women, maybe men and boys should get a fair chance to play ball? It's a metaphor.

24. Greatest Tennis Player of All Time I loved writing because tennis is my sport; I followed it all of my life and know it very well. I saw a photo of an aerial view of a decayed tennis stadium; that was all it took to again express my views on Pickleball (the Menace of Mankind!). Also, who was the greatest of all time? I like my choices.

25. Flog, Roval, Ring-Rong, Soccerball, Tri-Ball and a number of sports I've invented are on a New Zealand sports website. I've taken classic sports and *futurized them!* Here's how they should be played and might be played in the future? Imagine, there was never a game called golf. But there was FLOG and the greats of pro golf played flog. Who would win a Greatest of All Time match between Jack Nicklaus, Arnold Palmer and Gary Player, once called "the Big 3"? I enjoyed the art where I made it seem like the Big 3 each carried quivers that held floggers. If only dreams came true?

26. Story of Alfred E. Neuman just hit me. It was easy and I think the story covered a lot of bases in a short time...*IF there was a real dude mascot for Mad Magazine?* Easy for me, because I grew up on Mad Magazine. In fact, there actually was a real-person model they dressed up to look like Alfred E. Neuman at one point long ago in the magazine's early history. They had a tall guy made-up to look like Alfred and *he started to remove the clothes off a gorgeous, buxom babe.* I guess the image never left me? I'm sure it was for one Mad photo shoot and not like my story, where Alfie was a coked-up druggie who chased babes. Don't think Alfie was real. Maybe he was? Again, stuck for an ending until the end. What else? He went *mad!*

27. Pets. Aw, I got to show off a photo from 1981 of my beloved Eno. That pic was taken from my backyard in Bridgeville. I drove Eno all the way across country to California. He hated the drive, *the shaking~.*

28. Jose is a quasi-true story, parts are true. That's not Joe, we called Jose, in the picture. He wasn't Filipino or Hawaiian. He didn't play chess, write poems or play keyboards in a band. The dude was just a kid like the rest of us. He was athletic. A good-looking young man who had his pick of girls in our high school. He married hot, blonde, Dee Flint. They had 3 children. A terrible story of a downward spiral into heroin and hard drugs is also true. The man couldn't hold a job and was found by train tracks, dead. I felt I had to tell his sad story.

29. Homecoming. I found the photo on Pexels and I was intrigued by it and felt I had to use it. The story was almost autobiographical, although I was not in the military and certainly would never have fought in Vietnam. I knew the character (me) was dead on the battlefield and a ghost on the doorstep of home. I had no siblings and picked a film from 1972 (The Godfather). Rick Tolmer was a real person who died in high school for an odd reason. I apologize for making the Jimmy-character as dastardly as I made him out to be; he wasn't that bad. You might imagine the college scene of "Where's your pills?!" truly happened. *I was innocent!* I like the sudden end.

30. The Wrong Door was a fitting next story. I was sure I could weave a story around the image. The stories in

Storybook 4 were not written in the order of the Table of Contents. They were written in a jumbled order. I later saw some similarities like medieval times, Transylvanian themes and classic movies…so I rearranged them into an order where the stories flowed better, from one to the next one. Wrong Door went with death themes of the stories near the end. My idea was definitely influenced by *Carnival of Souls,* a creepy movie.

31. Saved turned out much better than I first conceived. Short and sweet. An obvious parallel to the Heaven's Gate cult. There *was* an object photographed that followed a comet in toward Earth, at the time of what became a "death-cult." Who knows? Mine was a joke.

32. The Death Chair. I happened to see that Frasier only because my computer went offline and I was stuck with free TV momentarily. The chair did resemble dad's old chair. And when the TV image showed the chair turned over, I got emotional…it was just how I found my father dead. I was moved to write about it. No, I never had a dream where I slipped him a tab of LSD. It would have been cathartic for him to have said the words I placed in his mouth and I wished I heard.

33. Where are you going? Now we come to funny stuff. Another story in a row that continues a Death-theme? What's your heaven going to be? What's *your* heaven going to be? Oh, you're not going to heaven? I see. If you saw the end of the movie *Betelgeuse*, then, maybe they got it right? We are all different and possibly our after-lives are also very different, individual and unique? In the case of my last story, I was told by an official source: *You cannot show female nipples!* I made sure not to show female nipples. It is alright to show cleavage, lots and lots of cleavage. When I found the perfect photo of a bus, it wasn't difficult to conjure up a funny story. Tele-Pyramids I had used before, they're time warps, you know? Not like the monoliths in *Time Bandits.* Why the girls weren't a little more kind to the dead dreamer is anybody's guess? He only provided perfection and utopia? Okay, I suppose utopia is relative? What's paradise to one person or one gender, might not be paradise to another person or the other gender, eh? Lesson learned. Oh, it's not Fred Rogers, it's Aaron Rodgers!

A swell way to end 33 stories. By my count, I've written over 200 short stories in my last 4 Storybooks. Each one with a neat color picture as a visual. Yes, I'm counting the short story of the cat who shits coins, why not? I'm very proud of the places I've gone with my mind and the places I've taken readers. Believe it or not, this entire book was written in 13 days: February 18th to March 2nd, today. Oscar night. The quicker I write, the higher the quality of the material. There's always polishing, correcting and adding small bits, but the stories and the comments were completed in less than two weeks. Unlike my other Storybooks, there is a flow to this one that pleases me and I hope will impress you. I stressed classics films and classic characters because we all know them, we're familiar with them. To give it an interesting twist or come up with a good sequel, is a difficult task. I use the expression: "sit down and write." I mean I sit down and IT JUST COMES. The longer I think, the more I go over and over it, the better it is. Maybe there's nothing else in my life? Or maybe I, at long last, have found the thing I'm best at and enjoy doing? There are parts of stories that no matter how many times I read them; I cry. My thinking is if I can put that much emotion in words, then maybe you'll feel it too and get something out of what I'm giving. Thank you.

Books written by TS Caladan (DH Jetson):

1) The Continuum
2) Son of Zog
3) The Cydonian War
4) Science-Faction [Vol. 1]
5) Science-Faction [Vol. 2]
6) ANAGRAMACRON
7) inspiration
8) 2099, Transia~
9) The New Men and the New World
10) Beyond Barronsland
11) Mandela Effect
12) Best of TS Caladan
13) Mandela Effect II
14) Collected Comedy of TS Caladan
15) TS Caladan's Comedy II
16) Pez Wars
17) The PEZ-Effect
18) Ceana
19) PEZ 4 Ever
20) My Cat Book
21) Artificial *Intelligense*
22) Teran Tales
23) Another Tera
24) Tera
25) 1001 Coincidences
26) Coincidences Continue*

27) 100 Very Short Stories
28) The Krown of Power
29) More Short Stories
30) Storybook Three
31) IF – The 4th Storybook

TS Caladan

Doug was born the only son of Rose and Steve Yurchey in Bridgeville, PA. in 1951. A loner, he drew pictures and dreamed of big/bright, colorful, fantasy-worlds that were inside the comic book adventures he cherished. Movies, TV, stories, art, thrilled the young man, especially sci-fi and anything that had to do with aliens and life on other planets. He grew up interested in sports and earned a half-scholarship in tennis to Edinboro State. After college, his interests turned to astronomy and various mysteries.

An unexpected event occurred: In 1973, he fell in love with a psychic who channeled. A three and a half-year marriage and a 'virtual Close Encounter' later, the young man was motivated to discover the truth in everything<. Odd occurrences happened during a strange marriage where spoons and keys bent with the powers of the mind. They met mentalist Uri Geller at this time. Wife Katrina did similar telepathic and "spoon bending" feats and their closest friends witnessed extraordinary things. In late 1977, the marriage ended.

Doug moved to LA in 1982. He worked on the Simpsons Show in 1990-1991 as a background "Clean-Up" artist. After 2000, he became a prolific writer with many online articles, radio interviews and YouTubes of his work on Atlantis, Nikola Tesla and the ancient World Grid. He was on 'Coast-to-Coast with George Noory' radio show and gave "the best interview since John Lear." Doug was filmed by National Geographic filmmaker Diego D'Innocenzo because of his theories on the prehistoric, rust-less,

TS Caladan

Iron Pillar in New Delhi. Nine million Italians saw the production on a TV Science show called 'Voyager,' with special-effects.

His writing dreams came true and he was published by TWB Press in 2015. Now *'TS Caladan,'* the author's interests are Modern Mysteries and conspiracies or secrets behind Hollywood and the Illuminati. Then he discovered the Mandela Effect in 2019, which *changed everything~.* Tray Caladan is a mystery himself. He has spent more than 50 years of pure, honest, scientific research and today uses artwork and wild/far-out, sci-fi stories to deliver his conclusions and positive messages...*and, still, no one believes him.* [A few do].

Contact information for Tray Samuel Caladan:
tscaladan@gmail.com

Questions and comments are very welcome. Readers will receive quick replies. Thank you very much.

~tsc

https://www.twbpress.com
Science Fiction – Supernatural – Horror – Thriller
and more

TS Caladan

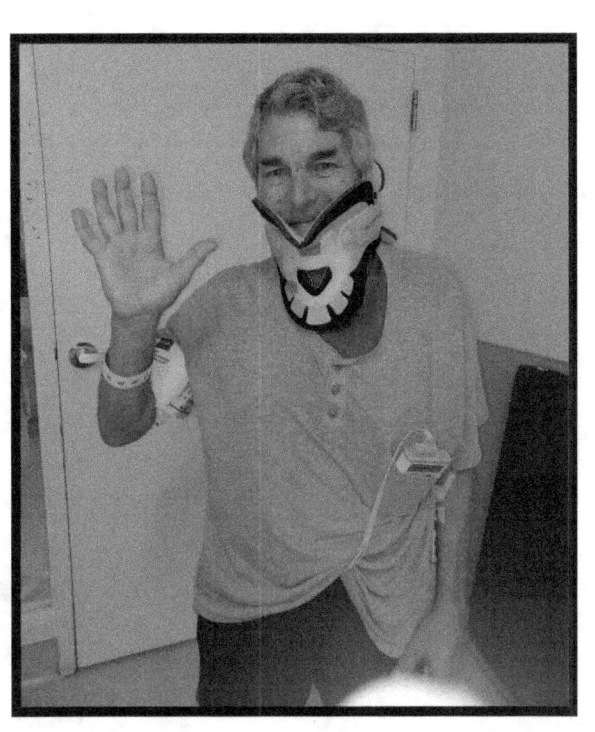

www.ingramcontent.com/pod-product-compliance
Lightning Source LLC
Chambersburg PA
CBHW071148260626
47162CB00003B/968